THE VENDETTISTS

A case of illegal dumping of toxic materials near his seaside home brings Colonel Charles Russell, former head of the Security Executive, out of retirement and up to London to see what can be done. Before long Russell is involved in far more than a local incident: with an assortment of colleagues and friends old and new, he is engaged in a tense and compelling battle to prevent not only a major Mafia crime, but also an ecological disaster.

THE VENDETTISTS

THE VENDETTISTS

by
William Haggard

MAGNA PRINT BOOKS
Long Preston, North Yorkshire,
England.

British Library Cataloguing in Publication Data.

Haggard, William
  The vendettists.

  A catalogue record for this book is
  available from the British Library

  ISBN 0-7505-0104-9

First Published in Great Britain by Hodder & Stoughton Ltd., 1990

Copyright © 1990 by William Haggard

Published in Large Print 1992 by arrangement with Hodder & Stoughton Ltd., London.

Printed and bound in Great Britain by
T.J. Press (Padstow) Ltd., Cornwall, PL28 8RW.

1

Colonel Charles Russell, lately head of the Security Executive, was quietly enjoying a semi-retirement. Leastleigh-on-Sea might not have been his private choice and had in fact been one of chivalry. For his housekeeper of thirty-three years' standing, a highland Scot who could still speak Gaelic, had unexpectedly begun to sicken. The London air had got to her lungs at last and the doctor had said that she would have to get out of it. Charles Russell hadn't hesitated a moment. She didn't wish to go back to her native glens, where by now she would be in effect a stranger, and to put her away in some home was unthinkable. But clean air she must have so Russell took her to Leastleigh.

Where the rather old-fashioned doctor had been proved right. In six months' time she was her old self again, a little shaky on her pins perhaps (he did the shopping and was well liked by the shopkeepers) but as active in mind as he was himself.

And Leastleigh wasn't a bad place to settle.

In Edwardian times extremely grand, it still had a pleasantly formal flavour. The big villas in the pompous avenues had mostly been turned into flats like Russell's but the shopkeepers were still polite and attentive, grandchildren running their grandparents' businesses. There was bridge at the golf club and Russell played there. It was bridge of a better-than-average standard but the players didn't take it too seriously. Charles Russell detested too-serious games of cards. There was a poker school too but he never joined it. All his life he had been playing poker, the stakes men's careers and reputations, sometimes their lives. To play it with pieces of pasteboard mocked the real world. And at last he had time for what he privately called educating himself. He had discovered the Victorian novelists but had decided that not all were divine. Or at least not divine all the time. But the minor ones like Surtees could make him laugh and as one grew into stoical disillusion laughter was an essential medicine.

And he still went to London once a week to lunch with the Executive's new head. Moreover these meetings were much more than nostalgic for the Executive was happy and often grateful to draw on his experience and flair. Most problems today had had earlier

8

precedents and Charles Russell was still both resourceful and ruthless. If the Executive had been a company his name would have been on the letterhead—Consultant.

This morning he had woken early; he usually did since he napped in the afternoon. He got up and made himself tea in the kitchen, taking it back to his bedroom to drink it. Then he shaved and dressed and went to the lavatory. He was blessed with regular bowels and used them. He picked up his daily paper from the mat. Dead on time as usual, he noticed. In Leastleigh the paperboys were entirely reliable especially if you tipped generously at Christmas.

He looked first at the stockmarket for he was fond of a flutter and had a nephew who was a stockbroker whom he used to translate his hunches into shares. Perhaps hunches was too crude a word for behind them lay logic and observation. Certain groups of shares were sometimes unfashionable, lagging behind the market as a whole, and when Russell was convinced of this he would ring up his nephew and give him a figure. Recently he had fancied the food giants so his nephew had bought him a thousand Unilever (and some for himself which he wouldn't have otherwise). The price had been ten-fifty-five, and following a split in

9

the holding he now had five thousand at four-seventy. Very nice. He was at present running a block of Electricals. They were slightly up but not a lot. He was sure they had more to go so he'd hold.

He then did the crossword without too much difficulty. With the news he hardly bothered at all. Even a major national like this one didn't carry, or maybe didn't dare to carry, what Charles Russell considered the real hard news. That he would get at his regular weekly lunches with Lord George at the Security Executive.

At nine o'clock he went to his sitting-room and at a quarter past was served with coffee. His housekeeper slept till half-past eight but Russell had no objection to that. He hadn't eaten breakfast for years and he knew that his housekeeper went to bed late; and at midnight precisely she'd start to drink. Quite a lot, he suspected, but he didn't demur. In the morning she was always sober.

'Good morning, sir.'

'Good morning, madam.'

They had been together for most of their lifetimes but their relationship had always been formal, master and highly respected servant. That is how both had always wanted it and a slightly exaggerated courtesy wasn't inapt.

Charles Russell drank his coffee contentedly.

Which was more than could be said of most men who had worked in the swink of what was loosely called Security. And his doctor had told him the week before that he was in really exceptional shape for his age.

The flat was the entire ground floor of one of the larger Edwardian villas and a well-kept garden ran down to a stream. On the further bank was a line of willows. The year before they had had to be pollarded, which had destroyed their elegant tracery but saved the trees. And in the undergrowth which grew around them there was still good cover for garden birds.

Russell wasn't a fanatic about birds, far less what was now called a twitcher; he never frequented uncomfortable hides, hoping to sight some exotic fowl; but his boyhood had been spent in the country and in really hard weather he put out food. And water—that was just as important. But he had an instinct for the animal life which mysteriously went its way around him. Or did he make his way around it? He didn't know. The year before a pair of mallard had nested in the little stream and their behaviour had astonished the flatowners. Notoriously wary birds, hard indeed to get a shot at, they'd behaved as though they'd been farmyard duck, waddling up to the back doors of the flats, begging for food and mostly getting it. They'd become almost hand-tame though never quite. And this year the pair of resident magpies were behaving very oddly indeed. It was late August by now and their brood was still feeding with them. They hadn't yet been driven away. There must be a reason for that, Russell thought. The epithet 'bird-brain' was the grossest misnomer. Birds behaved with their own but rigorous logic.

Today it was a flock of seagulls, wheeling and diving to pick up food. Charles Russell knew the reason for that: a fox had come in the night and turned over a bin. The gulls were feasting on what he had left them.

Gulls weren't Charles Russell's favourite birds. They were quarrelsome, particularly the blackcaps, and they were very dirty feeders indeed. But in the air they were magnificent, supreme. Russell had been reared in the Protestant ethic: if you did a thing you must do it well. Better if you did it superbly even if you had to stay up all night at it.

So he watched the gulls' unselfconscious mastery, wheeling and cruising, sometimes diving for the fox's leavings. All except one which was clearly in distress. It would turn but lose control, half-fall, fighting to regain flying height. It did this several times, then failed to. It hit the ground and lay there motionless. The

12

other birds paid no attention whatever.

Charles Russell went into the garden and picked it up. It fluttered feebly as he did so and then stayed still. He had expected to find oil on it, oil from some criminal's leak into the sea, but the bird was clean so it would be pointless to wash it. But it was certainly dying and dying miserably and Russell wondered how to despatch it decently. He had a shotgun but he didn't dare use it. The report would bring curious neighbours running and he'd be found to have shot a seagull. A seagull! They were supposed to carry dead sailors' souls and to shoot one was an act of impiety.

He decided he'd have to wring its neck and he hadn't wrung a bird's neck for twenty years... Green pigeon for the pot in India, partridge-walking them up in England. He had always declined to shoot driven birds and the thought of Edwardian battues made him wince. So he was out of practice but he'd have to do it... Very slight twist, then a firm strong pull. There was a barely audible crack and the bird was dead.

He couldn't leave it on the lawn so he took it inside. His housekeeper had seen him go out and had started to Hoover and dust the living-room. She saw the dead gull and said something in Gaelic, a language which Russell didn't know and in any case he misread her tone. He said on a note of unnecessary apology: 'I had to do it. The bird was dying.' She wasn't a sentimental woman and Russell had been a little surprised.

'I didn't mean that. I've seen animals die when they should have been put down before. I meant it was a crying shame.'

'Then what's the crying shame?'

'To see them poisoned.'

Charles Russell was surprised and showed it. 'You think this bird was poisoned?'

'I'm sure of it. Don't you read the local paper?'

'If you mean the two give-aways which they push through the letter box, the ones with the ads for the local loan sharks—'

'I meant the proper local newspaper, sir.'

'I'm afraid I don't.'

'If you did you wouldn't be asking questions. It's that tip at Queens.'

The full name of the village was Soken-le-Queen, but there were a Soken-le-Roi and a Soken Princes, so 'Queens' was the accepted usage.

'I didn't know there was one. What of it?'

'You'd know if you read the local paper. It's supposed to be for household rubbish but the paper says it's being fly-tipped with toxic waste.

14

The locals are up in arms to a man.'

'I can't say I blame them. But how does it happen?'

'The paper says the lorries sneak in at night.'

'With industrial waste?'

'So the paper says.'

'*Toxic* industrial waste?'

'You mean poisonous? The people of Queens say the smell's unbearable and you're holding a dead bird in your hand.' Her tone changed abruptly. 'May I ask what you're going to do with it, sir?'

'I'd thought of burying it.'

She clucked impatiently. 'In this East Anglian clay?' she had a long-serving servant's privilege of plain speech. 'You'd put yourself in bed for a week.'

He wasn't offended since he knew it was true. 'Then what are we going to do with it?'

'There's the dustbin.'

'Anti-social,' he said.

'I don't see why. Those lazy, overpaid dustmen come tomorrow and I'll wrap it in at least three bags.'

He watched her do so and took the package. Her duties were comprehensive and various but it had long since been agreed between them that it was the man who took the trash to the dustbin.

15

When he returned she had started to cook. 'What's for lunch?' he asked though he knew already.

'Salmon,' she said. 'Proper fresh salmon.'

He nodded approvingly for he never ate the other sort. There was a fishfarm quite near but its produce was suspect. A natural salmon's flesh was firm, whereas that of a farmed fish was not. It got its food too easily and his fishmonger, who greatly admired him, had let him into a little trade secret: a farm fish's food was doped to redden the flesh, and Russell was allergic to colourings.

It was a moment for a little flattery; it cost nothing and paid handsome dividends. 'My very favourite fish,' he said. 'Grilled with a little chives?'

'Of course.'

'And with that *hollandaise* sauce you make so brilliantly?'

'I've always called it sauce Montrose.'

'Then the people of Montrose eat well. The sauce you make in a double saucepan?'

'That's the one.' There was a fancy name for that double saucepan too but his housekeeper made *hollandaise* superbly without bothering her head with French.

He went back to the living-room and poured a sherry. He'd have to go carefully with alcohol

16

this morning since for once he was going to forgo his nap and take out the car in the afternoon. He didn't wish to lose his licence and the fact that the Chief Constable called him 'sir' wouldn't help him with the local beaks. So just one glass of sherry now and a single glass of white wine with the salmon.

Charles Russell was going to Soken-le-Queen.

He took his little car out after lunch. Once he had driven fast and for pleasure but now a car was a means of transport which, if he lost it, would change his way of life. He realised that he might still be tempted by the dangerous excitement of speed and had insured against its disastrous consequences by buying a very small car indeed. It had minimal power and no torque whatever but it did have four gears and Charles Russell used them.

He knew the way to Soken-le-Queen and though the site of the tip wasn't marked on the map he had rung up a local contact and been told. He drove away thoughtfully, deeply curious, for an ancient instinct was stirring uneasily. Something wasn't quite right at Soken-le-Queen.

He crossed the motorway by a bridge, drove four or five miles and turned left. Queens was less than a small market town but bigger than the average village for it was within easy reach of the marina at Layton to which yachtsmen came from as far as London. Some of them kept cottages here or put up at one of the two excellent inns; others slept on their boats but came to Queens for a solid meal. The village had the feel of prosperity.

Charles Russell drove halfway through it, then turned north. On the map the road tailed away into a track but he found that it was solidly metalled. For the first half-mile there were houses and bungalows, an overspill from the village proper, then these stopped and there was open land. It bore the usual crops of the East Anglian littoral, barley and rape and sugarbeet. The two former had been harvested and where the stubble had been fired it was smouldering surlily. But the beet still made an untidy green carpet. It wasn't a striking landscape nor beautiful.

Presently he could scent the sea, not the open sea with its tang and vigour, but the flat smell of what was a tidal estuary. He climbed a little rise and stopped, and the unlovely scene opened out before him. The estuary ran from east to west and at the moment it was very low tide. There was certainly more mud than water and beyond a bridge was a single island. Russell knew its name from the map, Sheeps Island, but he doubted if there were sheep there still. On his side of the water there had once been a jetty but this and its keeper's cottage had crumbled. It was a depressing, even a sinister prospect.

But Russell's prime interest lay in the bridge. The road where he'd stopped the car was still metalled and the bridge which continued it was surprisingly robust, a single-span affair of box girders. It was only one-track but that wasn't significant. It would clearly take a lorry or tanker.

Charles Russell restarted the car and drove on. At the bridge's mouth he stopped and got down. There was a notice which said PRIVATE PROPERTY and the bridge's entrance was sealed by a padlocked chain. Russell ducked under the chain and walked across. Here there was a concrete platform where the lorries presumably shunted to return, and on the far side of that a high chain-link fence. There were two wide gates but these too were padlocked. Another notice said simply: KEEP OUT.

He hadn't heard the man who'd come up to him for he'd moved silently on rope-soled shoes. When he felt his presence he turned and stared. The man was holding a loaded shotgun but it was broken, in the crook of his arm. But there wasn't a hope of a gamebird for many miles. Russell was startled and asked rather sharply: 'Are you that tip's guard?'

'I am not.'

The man had been staring at Russell in turn, taking in the worn old coat, the leather on the elbows and cuffs, the ancient handmade shoes. The inspection was thorough but in no way impertinent. He was one free man assessing another. Finally he took off his cap.

'Good evening, sir.'

'Good evening, Captain.'

'How did you know I could call myself "Captain"?'

'In the war I was in something called Combined Operations. That meant that I was on ships quite a bit. I can tell a seaman at sixty yards.'

'But the "Captain"?'

'If I may say so you have the air of authority.'

The other man led the way to a broken bench. His speech was a little hard to place: it wasn't quite gentle but nor was it rough, and there was a lingering hint of the local Doric. Before sitting he unloaded the shotgun, closing the breech and grounding it carefully, the muzzle pointing away from the bench.

'Never, never let your gun
Pointed be at anyone.'

Charles Russell nodded, reassured. This man was well accustomed to firearms yet he'd come where there wasn't a target.

Curious.

They sat down and the man said: 'Mathew Cole.'

'My name is Charles Russell.'

'A soldier, I'd guess.' Mathew Cole was an observant man.

'I soldiered till the end of the war, then I went into something they call Security. Now I'm semi-retired at Leastleigh-on-Sea.'

Mathew Cole had been smoking a small cheroot and had left the stub on the bench when he'd risen. He picked it up and tried to relight it; he failed and threw it crossly away.

Russell produced a leather cigar case. The cigars were already cut and pierced for he hated to carry unnecessary hamper. 'May I offer a smoke?'

'That's very civil.' Cole took a cigar but looked at it doubtfully. 'But this is going to be wasted on me.'

'If you enjoy it, it will not be wasted.'

'Aren't you smoking too?'

'I ration myself but this is an occasion.'

They both lit up and Cole said contentedly: 'This is beautiful tobacco.'

'Thank you.'

They had fallen into an easy companionship. Russell could see that Cole wanted to talk and Russell let him do so gladly.

He had enlisted as a boy in the Navy, rising steadily to CPO—Yeoman of Signals and any Captain's right arm. After the war he had taken his pension and had used his gratuity to tide him over while he qualified for his Master's certificate. Once he had it he had worked in cabotage, coastal freighters mostly based at Wivenhoe. That trade was decaying fast and he'd sensed it so he had bought himself a small boatyard at Layton. He looked after boats laid up for winter and there was a cabin cruiser which he chartered out to the few he felt were able to handle her. Sometimes he went as sailing master, sometimes not. And on the side he made a good deal in rescues.

He had laughed as he had explained the details. 'These estuaries are tricky waters and lots of the weekend sailors don't know their stuff. They go on the mud at high tide and want help. I've a flat-bottomed boat with a powerful winch so I go out and pull them off.' Cole laughed again; he relished the irony. 'An amateur on the mud at high tide doesn't quibble about the price of a refloat and afterwards I'm always tactful. When I've got them off I don't go back with them. I hang about for at least half an hour. There's nothing a weekend sailor likes less than being laughed at by the other amateurs. There are other men who do rescues too but I have the best reputation by far.'

Russell knew that the ice was broken and asked: 'So you do well enough to have time for shooting?'

'I employ two other men in the yard. I live with a widowed daughter and we live well. But I don't come here for the shooting, not really. There haven't been duck on these waters for years. I come here to shoot sick seagulls. I hate it. No seaman likes doing that, as you know, but I'd rather do it than see them suffer.'

'As it happens I had to kill one this morning.'

It was another strand in the thickening bond and Russell pointed at the gun on the ground. 'I thought you were guarding that tip,' he said.

'Nobody guards that tip—it's a scandal. An Inspector comes once a week but does nothing. He just opens those gates, looks round and goes. Meanwhile the cowboys come in unmolested.'

'Cowboys?'

'Unauthorised dumpers.' Captain Cole swore. 'That tip is meant for domestic rubbish, food-bags, old mattresses—that sort of thing. The foodbags burst and the seagulls feed on them. A seagull can eat most things and a little rotten food doesn't harm him. But industrial waste will poison him. Like you or me.'

'Those cowboys dump *toxic* waste?'

'They do. There's a proper disposal site for that but it's a long way away from the mid-Essex factories, so they save a good deal of mileage and time by sneaking in here. It's illegal, of course, and they come at night. But you can always tell when they've been by the smell. It makes you catch your breath and your eyes water.'

'But how do they get in?'

'With keys. They bribe some clerk in the District Office.' Captain Cole looked at Russell a little uncertainly; finally he decided to say it. 'Were you ever in India, sir?'

'A short time but too long.'

'My ship was sent there once when I was a boy. We were allowed shore-leave, though not much of it, but enough to find out how India worked. A backhander would fix anything and it seems to be getting the same way here. The petty officials are just as venal.'

It was a curious word for a Master Mariner

but Mathew Cole was by no means typical. Russell didn't comment but asked: 'So they slip in at night when nobody's here?'

'I came here once on chance and I happened to see one. A tanker, it was, and the two men wore gasmasks. I didn't and I had to leave quickly. But the tanker had an Essex number plate.'

'Anything recent?'

'I'd say a week ago. The smell lasts several days but has gone. But you've killed a bird and I've shot twenty.'

'Very ugly,' Russell said.

'It's criminal.'

'You've reported it, of course.'

'Of course. But what would you expect to happen? The junior clerks are deep in the racket and there was only my word for a pretty tall story. I got a letter back, quite polite, but it suggested I was an officious old busybody.'

The long summer evening had started to fade and Mathew Cole produced a watch. It was an old-fashioned silver watch on a chain. 'Time to be off,' he said, though reluctantly. 'I told you I lived with a widowed daughter and if I'm late for meals she creates.'

'I've a housekeeper who's much the same.'

Both men got up and Russell held out his hand. 'I very much hope we meet again.'

25

'I hope so too, sir. At the moment it's pretty quiet at the yard so I come here most evenings to smoke and think. And, of course, to shoot those wretched gulls. Come any evening you fancy but I don't think you should come at night.'

'Why should I want to do that?'

'You've as much social conscience as I have —maybe more. You might be tempted to catch a tanker dumping. Then there would be a second reporting and it would come from a better source than I am.'

'It's an idea,' Russell said.

'But not a good one.'

'Why not?'

'One of the crew of the last lot was swinging a cosh.'

'Fly-tipping under arms. That's new.'

'Suppose it had been a gun,' Cole said.

'I'd rather not. Why should it have been?'

'No reason at all. Just call it a foolish old seaman's hunch.'

'Not foolish at all,' Charles Russell said. 'I only wish I could think it was.'

He climbed into his car and drove away thoughtfully. A previous instinct had been disagreeably confirmed. There was certainly something wrong at Queens and it was unlikely that Mathew Cole knew the whole of it.

26

2

Next day was one for lunching with Lord
George so Russell took the train to London.
It involved one change from the local shuttle
but the trains were clean and some had buf-
fets. Liverpool Street was in temporary chaos
(temporary meant several more years) so he
walked up the steps to Bishopsgate and a taxi.
He had caught an early train and had time to
spare and moreover he wanted to stretch his
legs. He directed the cab to the Duke of York's
Steps and walked down them across the park
to Queen Anne's Gate.

Where the Executive had what it called the
front office. Nothing of importance was kept
there since nothing could be done effectively
to make a house like this one secure. The soft-
ware and the occasional file, the occasional
old-fashioned dossier, were kept in a modern
fortress in Ealing, but a web of electronic
wonders could put facts and often pictures
too on a screen in Queen Anne's Gate within
seconds.

In the taxi Charles Russell had considered

Lord George, for in the Prime Minister's absence he chaired the Executive and he ran its daily affairs as a matter of course. Russell thought him quite an admirable appointment. He'd been Foreign Secretary in a government which had unexpectedly fallen and the new Prime Minister, short of talent, had been tempted to ask him to cross the floor. But he had known that Lord George would not renege so he had appointed him Vice-Chairman of the Security Executive. Lord George had successfully defended his seat in the House but had been frustrated in opposition and miserable. He had applied for the Chiltern Hundreds at once and gone to the Executive gladly.

Where he ran a very tight ship indeed. Foreign affairs were meat and drink to the Executive, not the foreign affairs of dreary diplomats but the deadly affairs of international real politics. Lord George had had a headstart on those.

Russell was shown to his office directly and Lord George poured a handsome gin and tonic. He knew that Charles Russell preferred to drink sherry, but he had a liver himself and dared not touch it and Russell's own sherry was hard to come by. He noticed that his guest looked puzzled, staring over his head at the wall. There was a photograph of the Queen in

28

full fig and it hadn't been there on previous visits.

Lord George understood at once and explained. 'I know what you're thinking and so am I. The Queen is appropriate in messes and offices, places where the mandarins gather, but she isn't appropriate in a place like this. Which doesn't even appear in Whitaker and whose existence is hotly resented by the Left. It's in doubtful taste but an official issue. It was impossible to send it back.'

'Oh, quite,' Russell said but he hid a smile. That portrait on the wall was wrong, misplaced in more than the sense of bad taste. For Lord George had been born in a great Whig family and they hadn't forgotten the reverse feudal contract. The lady's ancestors had reigned by consent: they might obscurely sit on the throne of England, talking German amongst themselves as they pleased, just so long as the real business of government was conducted by the great Whig houses.

And very well indeed they'd done it.

They finished their drinks and went to Lord George's club. Its members were of a single party and Russell considered it rather dull. And the food was not as good as at his own. He was looking now at a piece of smoked cod's roe. It wasn't precisely off but it looked stale. Lord

George was ordering wine and not looking so Russell prodded the roe with a fork. It was hard. He squeezed out the lemon, hoping to soften it, then searched for the pepper pot. But he held his hand when he saw it was white. Slovenly, he was thinking. Poor catering.

Lord George had returned from the waiter and said: 'You're looking indecently well today.'

'I like to imagine I'm all right in the head.'

'Allow me to reassure you.' Lord George laughed. 'So anything of interest lately?'

Russell told him of the seagulls and the tip. 'The local papers are up in arms.'

'And it seems to have reached a national, too. A clipping came across my desk. I didn't pay much attention, of course. That sort of thing is not our business.'

Charles Russell thought this remark hubristic for his own experience had been quite to the contrary. Some trifle had crossed the same desk and he'd spiked it, and a fortnight later, quite out of the blue, it had been a recognisable piece of some political jigsaw. But he held his piece and listened to Lord George. He was off on another tack entirely.

'Have you heard of a man called Frank Loretto?'

'The head of the American Brethren? They

gave up funny names some years ago.'

'Funny names wouldn't suit our Frank at all. He wears sober suits which are made in London, he doesn't drink a lot or keep a mistress, and he runs the biggest racket in the world.'

'Drugs and gambling and women. I know.'

'And he's coming to London.'

'Is he indeed? The Commissioner won't like that at all.' Russell considered and then added thoughtfully: 'But London isn't Loretto territory.'

'The whole world is now Loretto territory. Except, I gather, the island of Sicily from which the Brethren originally came. I'm told that there's an open schism.'

'Interesting but not our concern directly. So why is he coming to London.'

'We wish we knew.'

Lord George began to explain it crisply. Women and gambling and drugs, they had said, so take women first. The Commissioner, who knew, was inclined to think not. There were plenty of prostitutes about, the porter of any big hotel would gladly give you a list of numbers, but it wasn't organised on the American scale, the old-fashioned pimp wasn't yet extinct, and to institutionalise what was still private business would take a lot of time and

31

money and might not show profits worth the effort.

'And gambling?' Russell asked.

Again different. The big establishments had their lids screwed on firmly. They were often clubs and therefore subject to club law and there was power to inspect and license them. Also they were reasonably straight. You could fiddle a deck of cards no doubt, but you couldn't control how a player called them. You could also tilt a roulette wheel slightly but that gave you only a doubtful advantage. It favoured one half of the wheel by numbers but the average gambler didn't play only *en plein*. He might choose a number, leave a small chip on it for as long as he played, but for most of the time he played the low yielders, the even chances or combinations. So the big rollers came back but there weren't many of them. And what a silly term that was! The big gamblers hardly even played craps. Above all there simply wasn't the volume to tempt a man like Frank Loretto. There was nowhere in the United Kingdom which seriously competed with Miami or Las Vegas.

So it had to be drugs?

The Commissioner feared so for the omens all pointed that way. The Brethren were in drugs already but they were far from having an English monopoly. America was bursting with heroin, close to saturation point, and it might be thought tempting to switch to Britain, to try for that elusive monopoly. That would be a double disaster—not only a huge increase in imports which could break services already strained but open fighting in the streets of cities as the Brethren fought for franchise and territory. It could be the Twenties in Chicago again and the Commissioner was right to fear it even more than he feared the organised smearing of his Force by the Left.

'But it could be something else,' Russell said.

'Like what?'

'I've no idea. I was stating a fact.'

'Not very helpful.' For once Lord George sounded less than urbane but he recovered quickly and went on smoothly. 'But you *could* be very helpful indeed.'

'Me? You are mocking me. I'm rather past doing anything active.'

'In anything above the eyebrows you're as good as you ever were or better. You have a vast experience and worldwide connections.'

'Gross flattery,' Charles Russell said.

Lord George decided to put his cards down but he played them carefully, one by one. 'I believe you know the Baron de Var.'

'I knew him very well in the war. He was

head of the Brethren in Sicily then and their collaboration saved a good deal of fighting. He's still nominal head but that means nothing. Real power in the Brethren has moved to America. Moreover, as you said yourself, there's something like a schism between the two. If you're thinking of sending me down to Sicily in the hope of getting some slant on Loretto, the idea is a total waste of time. De Var will be a very old man and he was always a cast-iron, old-fashioned Brother. He may hate Frank Loretto's guts and he may, just may, have received some hint of what is Loretto's intention here. But he isn't going to tell me that. No, sir. The old Brethren think the Americans decadent—they've never really approved of pushing drugs—but the last thing de Var will do is talk. *Omertá* and all that. It still operates fiercely.'

Lord George made no comment on this: it was true. But he laid another card down casually. 'And you're godfather to his only son.'

'Mario? Call it honorary godfather. I wouldn't call the de Vars over-pious but they've been Catholic for uncounted centuries and a Protestant godfather wouldn't have done. Especially as it was a rather grand christening with the local bishop and all the heavies.'

'Then why do you think they pulled you in?'

'It was shrewd. The boy's mother was an Englishwoman and she was going to insist on education in England. Someone trusted to keep an eye on that was going to come in very handy. And I assure you I took my duties seriously. So both at his prep school and later his public I took him out for exeats and so on and he sometimes stayed a night before he flew home.'

'Have you seen him since?'

'Oh yes, once or twice. He has friends here still and there have been funerals on his mother's side. He calls on me and takes me to luncheon. We always get on extremely well.'

'And, of course, he's a Brother.'

'I very much doubt it. It isn't a thing we've ever discussed. He isn't a prig and distrusts moral judgements—I taught him that—and to me he has never condemned his father. His attitude, if indeed he has one, I would describe by the single word "distaste".' Charles Russell drew a deep breath and summed up. 'So if he isn't a Brother he won't know a thing and if he is the usual rules will apply.'

'Logical—I admit it freely. But you will have to admit in turn that logic doesn't rule this particular chair. Or if it does, it doesn't rule absolutely.'

'You've a hunch?' Russell said. He respected hunches.

'I've a feeling that from a visit to Sicily you wouldn't come back quite empty handed.' Lord George could see that Russell was wavering; he could fight dirty and now threw a doubtful punch; he knew why Russell had left London for Leastleigh. 'Besides,' he said, 'it would be a break for your housekeeper. A few days on her own, you know.'

'I'm past air travel,' Charles Russell said. He had gone on a package tour the year before, as it happened to the east coast of Sicily, and the affair had been a complete disaster. It hadn't been a cheap tour either but everything had contrived to go wrong. The chartered aircraft had been late and shabby, the hotel overcrowded and its beach plain dirty.

Lord George could see he was nearly home. 'State your terms,' he said. 'We can probably meet them.'

'A first-class seat on a scheduled flight.'

'But of course.'

'A chauffeur-driven car to meet me and to be at my disposal throughout.'

'Agreed.'

'A good room in the best hotel in Cefalú. I take it that's where you'd like me to go since it's nearest to the Baron's home.'

'It's as good as booked.'

'I'll pay for my own drink, of course.'

Lord George allowed a smile and then a laugh. 'You were always a scrupulous man, dear Charles.'

'Perhaps that's why I've lasted as well as I have.'

The aircraft had been both punctual and comfortable and Russell used the time on it to refresh his memory of de Var and what the de Vars had stood for. Young Charles Russell had been in the Sicily landings but had shortly been lent to the American army. The reason had been a good one on paper for Russell was known to speak fluent Italian, but in practice it hadn't been good at all. Russell might speak Italian well but he didn't know a word of Sicilian. Which at one time had been an authorised language taught in the state schools as of right. Mussolini had changed that system in theory and the official language was now Italian. But it hadn't made much difference, then or now. As Russell had discovered on his visit the previous year. Italian might be taught in the schools, it was spoken by the head waiter and at the desk, but he had listened to two chambermaids nattering and he hadn't understood a word.

Nor had it made much difference in the war, for he and an American Colonel, something in Political Liaison, had been approached by two men who spoke passable English. They had worn dark suits and black fedoras and they had both been remarkably frank and open. They were Brethren who in effect ruled this island and they had excellent reason to hate all Germans. They were therefore proposing a sensible bargain. Give them arms and above all things explosives and they'd raise havoc behind the German lines. Bridges would go up and dumps and there would also be the occasional skirmish.

And the price? the American Colonel had asked. He had started at several million dollars, a very tempting sum in those days, but the Baron de Var had frozen instantly. Men of honour, he had explained with formality, did not take money for doing their duty. But there was a *quid pro quo* which the Colonel might offer. The Baron had colleagues in three states in America and all of them were in serious trouble. Four were serving unjustified sentences and several were threatened with deportation. If the Colonel thought that a fair exchange...

He had agreed at once and they'd shaken hands on it. Russell had doubted the Colonel's authority but the compact would save American lives, something the politicians would lap like milk.

In the event the Brethren's intervention hadn't caused the havoc de Var had promised but it had caused what good Resistances did cause, some confusion on lines of communication, some lessening in German freedom of movement. But the Germans had still fought stubbornly and well. Many had even escaped across the Straits to fight again up the spine of Italy. Charles Russell and others had resented this for by now the Allies controlled the sea. But the navies had been, well, rather naval. They had remembered the Dardanelles with a shudder. It was a sacrosanct doctrine that ships couldn't fight forts and the Germans had been clever with mines.

The lens of memory was sharpening steadily and Russell turned it on the Baron de Var. There'd been a time when the two men had met almost daily and Russell had slowly absorbed his background. The first de Var had been a Frankish Crusader, one of Bohemund's men from the *Gesta Francorum*. But his ship had never reached the Holy Land: instead it had inexplicably caught fire somewhere off the north coast of Sicily. It's captain and crew had been Greek and had panicked, seizing the lifeboats, abandoning the passengers shamelessly.

De Var had slipped over the side with his sword and had somehow struggled ashore, still belted. One of the lifeboats had got there before him and it had taken the ship's treasure chest with it. Men had broken it open and were already disputing. The Baron de Var had used his sword.

There'd been enough in the treasure chest to set him up comfortably and quite soon the de Vars had been local magnates. Thereafter the centuries had ticked away timelessly while the de Var lands swelled steadily into widespread *latifundia*. From magnates the family had promoted itself to potentates, Counts of the Holy Roman Empire. An Elector of the Palatinate hadn't thought it unseemly to give a daughter in marriage to the then Count de Var. And later had come the hated Bourbons, dispensing dubious Spanish titles and a rule which had been unmatched in brutality. The de Var was now the Marquis of Something but his descendants still called themselves plain Barons de Var. For by now they were quintessential Sicilians, mistrusting all foreigners, Italians included, proud and independent and dangerous.

The aeroplane had landed safely and the gangway had been towed up to the door. Charles Russell was waved through Customs and Passport Control. It was short of the full red-carpet treatment but he was clearly expected and treated respectfully. In the concourse he saw Mario de Var.

'Good morning, sir.'

'Good morning, Mario. I didn't expect you. I have a car.'

'I've ventured to send it back to your hotel. If you don't object I'll take you there myself. I want to talk and that won't be easy either at the hotel or at home.'

'I'll be glad of a chance to talk,' Russell said. It was more than a polite rejoinder for he was here as Lord George's eyes and ears.

They had slipped back at once into an easy friendship for they'd been closer than Russell had told Lord George. If Russell had had a son he'd acknowledged he would have liked him to be a Mario de Var. Both men were on the face of it extroverts, fond of the good things of life, companionable; and both men at times felt the need of privacy, withdrawing into private values behind an impeccable but impenetrable courtesy.

Mario led the way to a near-vintage Rolls. He was driving himself and Russell sat beside him in front. Mario had difficulty finding first gear. 'Dreadful old car,' he said. 'A right bitch. You have to double declutch all the time or strip the box. And power steering hadn't been thought of when this thing was made.'

'This thing' slightly grated on Russell. He had once owned a Bentley not dissimilar. 'What you should do with this thing,' he said, 'is put it in one of your barns, jacked up. Cover it with a plastic sheet and let it be for a few years more. When you go to it next you'll discover a fortune.'

'And what do we use for transport till then?'

'I hear that FIAT's paintwork has much improved.'

'Father still likes an airing occasionally.' It was spoken with an affectionate irony. 'And though we're not exactly begging bread we're no longer the wealthy family we were. We have land in the north still though it's not very profitable but the great estates in the south have gone. Have you read *The Leopard?*'

'A long time ago.'

'We once lived like that: it was classically feudal. But after the war they broke the estates up, "they" being the Italian government. Now there are yeomen and state collectives. Maybe it had to come—I don't know—but the way it was done left us all very bitter. There was envy, hatred and malice in all of it. I gather you had the same thing in England.'

'We did have Labour governments, yes.'

42

'It was all done by legislation, of course, and it provided for reasonable compensation. But the civil servants concerned were mainland Italians and men of the Italian Left. Naturally they fiddled the values and what we got was next to nothing.'

Charles Russell saw a chance to probe. He didn't like the need to do so but he was here in the sun on the Executive's money. 'But your father will have other means.'

Mario thought this over for a mile. Finally he said carefully: 'You are referring to the Brethren?'

'Yes.'

'I dare say they give him a modest pension but he's long past active participation. He's respected for what he was but that's all.' Mario hesitated but then when on. 'And talking of the Brethren, people have the strangest idea of them, especially of what goes on in Sicily. Would you care to hear the history?'

'Yes, please.'

So originally the Brethren had been a sort of Resistance, guerillas against the horrors of Bourbon rule. Did some Spanish sprig seduce a local? Then quite shortly he would die rather nastily and there'd be no sort of charge to the unhappy girl's father. Mario said much the same thing as his father had said to the

43

American Colonel. Men of honour wouldn't consider money when doing what they saw as a duty.

Russell knew there was some truth in this. Not a lot but it was a supportable statement. The Brethren by now were indisputably evil but like all evil men did good occasionally. 'Things have changed a bit since then,' he said.

They had indeed but at first rather slowly. The next move had been into simple extortion. Here in the north there was water to spare but in the south it was scarce and vital to land-owners. The greatest of Spanish grandees was helpless when his water-channels were quietly sabotaged. But the greatest changes had come from outside as the world had changed its way of life. The Brethren who had emigrated to America had started with a clean sheet and misused it but Sicily had changed too though more slowly. It was by no means fully in-dustrialised yet but it was no longer an agricultural slum. The population had risen sharply, there were great cities and ports and even some industry.

In this year of disgrace there was also tourism and the tourists went home and complained of the Brethren. Entirely wrongly: they'd been in no way concerned. Some woman had her handbag snatched and complained to the police that a Brother had done it. Ludicrous if you knew the facts. The Brethren weren't concerned with street crime: they deplored it since it was bad for the tourist trade. They were too busy with their traditional businesses, gambling and women and, of course, extortion, putting the bite on the big hotels. They could even put the bite on FIAT.

...But every now and then, in the papers, you'd read that Rome had broken the Brethren.

You were credulous if you believed a word of it. Some police chief would be sent down from Italy and reinforcements of *carabinieri*. Between them they'd round up some of the small fry and maybe a few in the middle echelons. The really big boys went untouched as they always had been. The mayors of two of the biggest towns were secretly very senior Brothers. That was the position here, the Brethren conducting their almost-tolerated rackets. In America it was very different. In America there was a vast empire built on drugs.

Charles Russell saw the chance of another probe. 'I gather you're not a Brother yourself.'

Mario laughed though without amusement. 'Nine years in England at English schools disqualified that horse at the gate. Not even Father could have got me in.'

'Do you resent it?'

'I did at first. It's hereditary and I'm a de Var. But I don't resent it now a bit. With things degenerating the way they are I'm glad to be out'

They were driving past the new FIAT complex and Mario took a hand off the wheel to point. The car almost went off the road but he pulled it back. 'It gives employment, I suppose, and that's good. It is also more potential victims.'

'You're hiding something,' Russell said.

'We need a drink.'

They turned right off the motorway and under it, through a lighted tunnel, towards a cluster of bleak apartment high-rises. 'The FIAT workpeople live in those but there's still a village outside the ring.'

They drove through the concrete fortresses to what had once been a small coastal port. There was a café on the abandoned quay and they sat down. They ordered cold beer and drank it gratefully.

Mario said: 'Can I trust you, *padrino?*' He very seldom called Russell that.

'If it's not against my country's interest—'

'No.'

'Then I think that you could safely trust me.'

Mario let his breath out slowly and Russell read the gesture correctly. It was more than one of relief: he was being thanked. 'I've got to get this off my chest. I thought of a priest but a priest would be useless. He could only tell me I'd committed no sin. I know that already but I'm worried to death.'

'Start at the beginning, please.'

'I will. You remember I told you I wasn't a Brother. Also that I was glad of it. Because the Brethren are doing something which breaks the rules. Not the people here whom we more or less tolerate but the American Brothers, the big boys in drugs. They've started to pump drugs into Sicily. That's something new and quite unacceptable.'

'You're not telling me there weren't drugs here before?'

'Of course there were but the trade was manageable. In the nature of things there were quite a few addicts and the tourists were an additional market. But an organised campaign of pushing would be hell.'

That was something to take home, Russell thought; Lord George and the Commissioner would be delighted to hear it. The next big target would not be Britain, or at any rate not as a target for drugs. He considered for some time, then asked: 'And what does your father think of that?'

'He thinks of it as fouling one's own nest. He was always against the Brethren handling hard drugs. The traditional things were quite all right but trading in cocaine was not. Peddling drugs wasn't work for gentlemen and when the Americans built it up as big business he was very disapproving indeed. But there was nothing he could do to stop them and he salved his elastic conscience easily. The American people were already degenerate and if they chose a quicker descent into hell than would otherwise have been inevitable that wasn't a matter to be held against Father. But many of the American Brethren were Sicilian by blood and origin and to corrupt your own people was a very grave sin. Worse, it was a dishonourable act, something outside the code, unforgivable.' Mario looked at Russell unhappily; finally he said very quietly: 'My father is old-fashioned and orthodox, and the shame of it is poisoning his old age. That dishonours me too.'

Nine years in English schools, Russell thought, and he's still a patrician Sicilian, unredeemed. 'You said they'd started to pump in already. How do they do it?'

'They do it by air. It's brought in from Spain and the aircraft is refuelled here. Their own

48

men come with it and flog the drugs. When one load is finished they go to ground in Palermo, waiting for another consignment. All of them are Loretto's men.'

'Loretto,' Russell said on a reflex. The name Loretto seemed to be everywhere in America; visiting England; and now here.

Mario had caught the note of surprise. 'You've heard of him?' he asked.

'Who hasn't?'

Mario said: 'I've got to stop him.'

'I sympathise with your point of view but isn't that a pretty tall order?'

'I can think of a way if I had the arms.'

'Some of the locals would help you shoot it out?'

'Not that.'

It was on Russell's tongue to ask: 'Then what?' but Mario de Var had risen. 'Now I'll take you to the hotel,' he said. 'I've checked the arrangements your own people made for you. The room you had was not the best but now they've given you one with a sea view. And the food looked rather better than average. I've spoken to the head waiter, naturally.'

'You're extremely kind.'

'A personal pleasure.'

They climbed into the old Rolls and drove away. They didn't speak again till they reached the hotel. Where Mario said: 'A word of warning. Father is pretty old, you know. I wouldn't call him strictly ga-ga but he has days and he has other days. When I told him you were coming to lunch he was delighted. But if it's one of his other days he won't know you.'

'Embarrassing if he doesn't.'

'Not at all. Father still has beautiful manners and will assume that you're a guest of my own.'

'I hope it's a good day.'

'So do I. Father likes to lunch early, at half-past twelve, and it's only twenty minutes to the house. So calling at twelve would give plenty of time but if I may I'd like to come earlier and use the hotel pool. I take it you'll be using it too.'

'I certainly shall.'

Mario wrestled with first gear and got it in. 'Then I'll see you at the pool.'

Charles Russell ate his dinner and went to bed. Normally he slept eight hours like a baby, able to occlude his worries, and when he suddenly woke in the small hours he knew at once that he wasn't alone. The man was moving with professional quietness but the pencil thin beam of his torch was visible.

Russell lay still and thought deliberately. He

was unarmed and no match for a younger man but reason suggested that he wasn't in danger. If this man had intended to kill he'd have done so already. Much simpler to search with a dead man in bed than a live. But why was he searching at all and for what?

Wait and see. Charles Russell lay perfectly still till the man had gone. It wasn't easy but he had steady nerves.

When he heard the faint click of the bedroom door shutting he gave it five minutes and then turned on the light.

His passport and travellers' cheques were in the hotel safe but his small change which he'd left out had gone, as had his watch and an almost valueless lighter. Also missing was a pair of silver-backed hairbrushes and his keys had been used to open his briefcase.

A very poor night for some petty hotel thief.

Russell didn't go back to bed but sat in a chair. He knew he wouldn't sleep again and he needed to do some serious thinking.

...Some petty hotel thief? Say twenty to one. But he was also Charles Russell of the Security Executive and he'd been received at the airport with considerable respect. That was explicable: Mario would have dropped a hint. And he'd been seen to drive away in the Baron's car. So the local Brethren had no reason to fear him,

51

certainly none to search his room.

There remained the rank outsider which occasionally, just occasionally came in. In this case its name was Frank Loretto. He, Russell, was what he was or had been and his movements both here and in England had not been concealed. His briefcase had been opened fruitlessly for it had held nothing but his documents of travel. Frank Loretto was known to have men in Sicily...

A very long shot but the horse was a runner. The immediate question was what to do and the answer, inescapably, nothing. It was his duty to report a theft but the last thing he wanted was police enquiries. If he told Mario it might dry him up and almost certainly he had more to give. He wouldn't even tell Lord George when he got home. Lord George would think he'd gone over the hill.

So that was that except for one thing. He was furious about those hairbrushes. They had been given to him by his father on his twenty-first birthday and now he wouldn't see them again. What he'd heard of Loretto had not inclined him to like him but if this apparently petty theft were more than it seemed, if this wild outsider had really won, then somewhere in the account to be settled would be an item of two pieces of silver.

3

Charles Russell had ordered tea at seven o'clock. It came punctually as he showered and shaved, then he went downstairs in search of coffee. Normally he didn't eat breakfast, but he looked at the croissants, was tempted and fell. He pottered round the garden a while, then went upstairs to change for the pool. By ten it was already hot.

He slipped into the big pool and began to swim. He still swam strongly and enjoyed the exercise. When he had had enough he climbed out. He dried himself and put on a beach robe, then he sat in the warm shade for he hated the sun. He had had a bad night and he dozed contentedly for its events he had put firmly behind him.

When he woke he saw that Mario had arrived. If he had seen his godfather he hadn't disturbed him but gone straight to a cabin and changed into swimming trunks. He was standing on the diving board now, collecting himself for the first dive of the morning.

Russell watched him as he balanced his body.

He knew that he'd had an English mother but her blood had not diluted his figure. He was the typical Mediterranean man—heavy shoulders and powerfully-muscled arms. On a north European his legs would have looked two inches short, but English legs would have made him look top heavy. As he was he looked compact and powerful. Russell knew he'd been born to a second marriage when his father had been in his middle fifties. That put Mario in his forties somewhere. Mario de Var bore his years with grace.

He made his dive and began to swim, and Russell saw that he did it extremely well. He did maybe a dozen lengths in an effortless Olympic crawl, then turned on his back where he was almost as fast. He wasn't showing off in any way; he was having an enjoyable swim. He did a few lengths of the backbreaking butterfly, then climbed out. He saw Russell and came over smiling.

'Good morning, sir.'

'Good morning, Mario.'

Mario found another chair and pulled it up by Russell's but in the sun. He can take it, Russell thought; it gives me a head. 'You swim superbly,' he said.

Mario laughed. 'I'm competent in the water perhaps, but it's the only sport I'm any good at. At school I was quite hopeless at games. I tried the lot—both sorts of football, cricket and tennis. I was a laughing stock at all of them. So I took to the water.'

'Do you do a lot of swimming still?'

'Not as much as I'd like to because I have to use the hotel pools. Since two of them stand on land we once owned they don't make too much fuss about that, but it's not the same thing as having your own pool.' He added a little wistfully: 'We had one once, Father built for Mother, but when she died he let it go.'

'But knowing that you were fond of swimming...'

Mario allowed a Latin shrug. 'Sicilians aren't very fond of water. I suspect they think swimming is slightly unmanly.'

'Maybe it is but your sort isn't.' Russell looked at the clock on the roof of the changing room.

'Yes, it's time we changed. You could have a drink while we're doing it, too. That is, if you want a hard drink before luncheon. Father doesn't keep spirits except some brandy and you won't be drinking that before a meal. What you'll get is Marsala and local wine. It comes from one of the co-operatives which took over from the great estates and I'm bound to say they've much improved it. But then they had government money to do it.'

'I'll be perfectly happy with Marsala and wine.'

'Then I'll go and change.'

They drove through the coastal strip for a couple of miles. It was being developed with villas and small hotels, neither town nor open country, and hideous. Presently they reached rock-strewn fields and Russell could feel that they had started to climb. Quite soon they saw Castel de Var before them and they drove through its narrow streets to an arch in a wall. Beyond it was the central square, at its southern side the castle itself. It was more of a keep than a formal castle—Norman, Russell guessed, and beautifully kept; and it had more the air of a home than of a monument. A long flight of steps led gracefully to a terrace along the front. They climbed them deliberately, holding the handrail, and sat down on a padded wooden bench. A servant brought Marsala on a crested silver tray. Mario de Var said formally:

'My father's apologies but he will receive you at luncheon. He's having a pretty good day as it happens but he does have to husband such strength as is left to him.'

The terrace was in the shade and comfortable, and they sat and watched the scene before them. Beyond the curtain wall, once defended,

56

the village had grown by natural accretion, countrymen seeking the keep's protection against Greek pirates or Arabs or the Bourbon terror. Over the uncounted centuries a settlement had become a village and was growing into a small market town. Russell had brought glasses and used them. There was a tented camp beyond the village and Russell didn't believe what he saw.

Mario had noticed his astonishment and explained. 'Yes, it's a giraffe, all right. That's the winter headquarters of the local circus. It's out on the road at the moment, naturally, but for that it uses caravans and it leaves what it doesn't want behind. And it doesn't want that giraffe. It's sick.'

'I'm sorry to hear it,' Russell said. A sick giraffe in Sicily could hardly be a happy animal.

'They'll treat it well enough till it dies but I hear that they don't intend to replace it. People stare at it but it doesn't pay. On an elephant you can put a howdah, making money taking children for rides. You can't train up a giraffe to do that.'

'And bolting they can do forty easily.'

They dropped their eyes to the square below them. It was market day and the scene was dazzling, the crowd breaking and reforming again into patterns which defied choreography.

57

The stalls were busy with local trafficking, countrymen and countrywomen selling their own produce happily, taking in each other's washing. One stall in three was clearly alien, a pedlar's from some neighbouring town. These sold gimcrack crockery and rubbish generally and they didn't seem to be doing very well. The citizens of Castel de Var were enjoying themselves at their weekly treat but they hadn't lost their peasant frugality. They had an experienced eye for trash and let it lie. An occasional gypsy stalked by indifferently.

To the left of where Russell and Mario sat was the door of a church built into and beyond the wall. There was a wedding going on, with music, and presently the couple came out. They stood under the arch which had fine dog-toothed moulding and the crowd cheered and whistled. Cameras began to click and there was a shower of confetti and then of rice. A sour-looking priest had appeared behind the newly-weds. Mario said: 'He won't like that.'

'All that paper to clear up?'

'No, the rice.'

'It's no worse than the paper.'

'It is to him. It's also a pagan symbol—anathema. He's bigotted and a bit of a boor. I'm afraid you're going to meet him at lunch since he's also Father's private chaplain. Myself he has long given up as lost. All those years in that thrice-damned heretical England...'

A second servant had come out to the terrace. He appeared to be the majordomo for he was dressed in a morning-coat and carried a wand. He bowed and said in antique Italian: *'Che i signori s'accomodino.'*

They went into the house, up more steps, and finally into what had been the great hall. The windows were narrow embrasured slits and the room must once have been lit by rushes or lamps. Today two candelabra were blazing.

The Baron was in a wheelchair, sitting upright. He looked older than Russell had expected to find him, frail, on the final lap of existence. But he recognised Russell and he wasn't pretending.

'My very dear Charles! It is kind of you to have come all this way.'

There was a man behind the Baron's wheelchair in the dark trousers and long white coat of a male nurse, and he slowly manoeuvred the Baron to the table. His chair was a fine old piece of oak but on one side the arm had been sawn away. The nurse pulled the Baron de Var half-upright, then neatly slid him sideways onto the chair. The Baron very slightly groaned. The priest had appeared from the shadows and said grace. Russell and Mario, who'd been standing,

59

sat down. The nurse had quietly slipped away but the majordomo stood motionless behind the chair. The meal was served by a liveried servant. Except for the electric light the centuries had slipped by unnoticed.

The Baron had groaned as he sat but had recovered. He began to talk of old times with surprising lucidity, but he did it with certain reserve. Much of what he had contrived with Charles Russell was secret still and a part was disreputable. But events were in the right order and he remembered names. It was a bravura performance and Russell admired it. From time to time he fed lines to the Baron, but the other two men at the table said nothing. Mario was watching his father and the priest was too busy eating noisily.

Russell, who'd spent his boyhood in Ireland, recognised the type at once. He would be the product of some local seminary, orthodox, bitter and unforgiving. He had probably joined some minor Order for it was certain that none of the great ones would take him. There'd been a priest in *The Leopard*, Charles Russell remembered, who'd been advised to take a bath more often. This one, as it happened, didn't smell but in other ways was as unattractive. Hair grew out of his ears in fierce thickets and his soutane was stained by the droppings of many meals. He ate like an animal, head down and greedily, swallowing great chunks of *polpo*. He was a half-educated peasant—dangerous. Yet those mourning-nailed hands could work deathless miracles...

Charles Russell reined his thinking sharply. For a Protestant Anglo-Irishman it wouldn't do.

The Baron had begun to fade, not noticeably at first, but increasingly. He'd had an English-woman as his second wife and had no doubt learnt some English from her, but that had been some years ago and up to now he had been speaking Tuscan. Now he'd begun to slip into Sicilian; he needed prompting on names and dates; his head nodded.

His son made a signal to the waiting major-domo who left the room. Presently he returned with the nurse and together they got de Var back into the wheelchair. It was a harder task than getting him out of it for the Baron was no longer conscious.

But he rallied as they pushed him past Russell's chair. His head came up and his eyes were alive again; he said in very passable English:

'Goodbye, old friend. We shall not meet again.'

The priest had slipped away to sleep and Russell would have liked to follow him. But Mario led him back to the terrace. There were coffee and brandy on separate tables and the liveried servant behind them, waiting.

'Coffee and brandy?'

'Just coffee, thank you.' Russell had drunk several glasses of wine and it had certainly been improved enormously. Also it had become much stronger. His idea of spending the afternoon was a comfortable chair in the shade and silence. But he had sensed that he wasn't going to get either.

Mario wanted to talk and said: 'I'll drive you up into the hills where you fought.'

'I'd like to very much indeed.' It was a social lie and quite inescapable. Guests didn't dictate how their hosts entertained them.

They drove away again in the noble old car and this time the ground began to rise steeply into the spine of hills which fringed the north coast. Locally they were called 'the mountains' but in most of the other countries of Europe they wouldn't have rated more than big hills. Russell remembered them as quietly pastoral semi-alpine meadows with flowers and sheep. Or there had been sheep till the two armies had eaten them. There had been smallholdings and these seemed to have disappeared. But the magpies were there still, indestructible, and Russell murmured the ritual 'Good morning' three times. Superstitions, he had long since decided, were a matter it was safer not to despise.

Mario de Var was talking continuously and normally he wasn't garrulous. Russell sensed that he was for some reason nervous and wondered why. He put it behind him for he'd very soon know.

Mario pointed at a hilltop village. 'That's deserted,' he said, 'there's nothing moving. Once it was a prosperous mining community but South American ores put it out of the market. So the people have all gone down to the coast. Its development has ruined a beautiful coastline but if it wasn't for the new factories like FIAT those people would starve.' He turned to Russell unexpectedly. 'Do you know where we are, sir?'

'No. But if you could find a sort of bald-headed hill, where the earth has slipped away from the rock—'

'Where the last battle was fought?'

'That's the one.'

It had indeed been a considerable battle, a foretaste of later events at Caserta. It had been impossible to outflank the fortress so they'd had to take it by frontal assault. American

63

aircraft had bombed it mercilessly, day in, day out. But when the attack had gone in the Germans had still been there. They had fought bitterly against superior forces before retreating to the coast in good order. Where they hadn't been so fortunate as their brothers to the east of them, no Straits of Messina but open sea, no organised ferries but only fishing boats. These they had seized and put out to sea but very few had reached the mainland.

Mario drove on till the hill was visible. 'I'm afraid there's no road up,' he said.

'I remember that very well indeed. And a few miles on there was an American airfield. They called it a TAA—Tactical Advanced Airstrip. It wouldn't take the bigger aircraft but it would take groundstrafe fighters and lighter bombers.'

'Would you care to revisit it?'

'I think I would.'

They drove on again till Mario stopped. He pointed to the valley below them. There'd been a shower and the airstrip's tarmac glistened in the sun. 'It's a winding road down and I've no power steering.'

'I'd like to go down just the same if you can.'

Mario drove down in bottom gear, pulling the massive old car round the curves. At the bottom was the strip, now drying.

'It looks in pretty good shape,' Russell said.

'The Americans keep it that way. Not the American Air Force now but the Americans who are bringing in drugs. This is where their aircraft land. To add insult to injury this airstrip is on our land.'

Russell remembered a previous conversation. Mario had cut it short rather suddenly... 'I've got to stop him.'

'I sympathise with your point of view but isn't that a pretty tall order?'

'I can think of a way if I had the arms.'

'Some of the locals would help you shoot it out?'

'Not that...'

Then what?

Russell had taken an immediate decision, the quicker since it was also familiar. For the ethos of the Security Executive had been its own. The law was no doubt a braying ass but it held up the pillars of any civilised society. Step outside it too casually and you brought down the rafters. Certainly—that was accepted thinking. But the inescapable facts of real life remained. There'd been that junior Minister in the Ministry of Defence who had suddenly become exceedingly rich. There'd been evidence but it couldn't be used since to do so would have brought down a government. Or that Trades

65

Union leader, an unashamed syndicalist, who had nearly succeeded in destroying an industry. One had been known to need adrelanin regularly and one morning they'd found him dead of an overdose. The other had been driving fast when his steering had inexplicably broken.

There'd been men who'd been willing to do such things and when, on occasion, they'd been caught they hadn't complained. They had gone to prison stiff-lipped and silent. The community had found them criminals but as men they were in no way dishonoured.

And drug-running was an enormous evil, arguably greater than selling state secrets or planning to bring an economy to its knees.

At the other end of the still serviceable runway were the ruins of the old control tower. It had been built of alien bricks and had crumbled. Its roof had fallen in and its windows stared blankly. It had been well behind the line of battle but would certainly have had the means to defend itself. Charles Russell nodded: they might still be there. An outside chance but there it was. For the Americans had been profligate with their arms; they hadn't been obliged to husband them and sometimes had been decidedly careless.

'When Loretto brings his planes in here I

take it they don't use that control tower.'

'Any gear in it has long since been looted.'

'I wonder,' Russell said.

'Wonder what?'

He didn't answer directly but asked in turn: 'Have you a crowbar?'

'No, but I've got a spade. Sometimes in winter when there's mud—'

'Then bring your spade.'

They got down from the car and walked towards the ruined tower. The swimming had done Charles Russell good and he walked easily, with a spring in his step. At the gaping door of the tower they stopped. Inside it they could see piles of rubble.

'Looks pretty dangerous,' Mario said.

Charles Russell didn't answer but ducked inside.

The broken windows gave adequate light and he leant on the spade and looked around. The concrete floor which had never been thick had cracked in a mosaic of gothic complexity and on it lay white dust from the ceiling. Russell prodded with one point of the spade. In most places it sank in two or three inches.

He began to quarter the floor methodically, obliged to avoid the piles of rubble but covering the rest in longitudinal sweeps. The point of the spade went in and out almost soundlessly but presently there was the ring of metal. Charles Russell let his breath out quietly, he made a cross on the ground where the spade had struck and handed it to Mario de Var.

'Will you clear away the debris round that. You'll find a plate.'

Mario did it quickly and neatly and then stood back. They were looking at a slab of steel, perhaps eight feet long by six feet wide. At one end was a countersunk ring.

'That means it's hinged at the other end.'

'I'm to open it?'

'If you can. There's probably an air-seal, though.'

Mario bent his strong legs and pulled. Nothing gave.

It was useless for Russell to try to help him. The ring would take only one pair of hands and Mario was by far the stronger man.

Mario took off his coat and shirt, showing his powerful shoulders and biceps. He tried again and again nothing moved; he stood upright for a moment and rested. Russell could see that he'd started to sweat. He gathered his strength and pulled again.

This time there was an audible pop as the seal broke and the air rushed in. The counterweighted plate swung up on its hinge.

Now they were looking at a considerable

armoury, three lines of weapons in carefully spaced rows. Those furthest from Russell looked like plastic soup plates. Mario had already knelt but Russell said sharply: 'Don't touch those. They're anti-personnel mines, horrible things. Set one off and there's a smallish explosion. That blows the main charge upwards, say two feet. When that explodes in turn you've lost your legs.'

'Would they stop a landing aircraft?' Mario de Var asked the question unhesitatingly. He had told Russell how the drugs came in and he had told him that he would stop them if he could. Russell would never have led him to these arms if he'd been anything less than sympathetic.

'They might—I don't know. But it's hardly relevant. To use them you'd have to bury a row of them and that tarmac outside looks pretty solid. And you'd need more tarmac to cover what you've done. Let's see if there isn't something more suitable.'

Russell got down on his knees in turn, taking something from the second row. It was carefully wrapped and Russell undid it. 'Anti-tank rifle,' he said. 'Quite obsolete. They were useful in the early days, particularly against your own absurd armour, but were futile against anything German. They were

69

discontinued as useless.'

'But wouldn't it stop a landing aircraft?'

'I doubt it. Solid shot, you see. It would go through the windscreen and kill the pilot but it wouldn't destroy the aircraft nor its load. Let's see if third time's luckier.'

He took a specimen from the third row of weapons. It was heavier and Charles Russell was kneeling. Mario had to help him lift it. This one was in a plastic bag. Russell tugged at it but it didn't give. 'Have you a knife?'

Mario had put his coat back on. 'Only the one I've carried all my life.'

'Have you indeed? Then give it to me. Once you've made a slit and have something to hold, that plastic should tear away quite easily.'

Mario gave him the knife and Russell tore. The cover was rather stouter than he'd thought and he had to make two incisions, one each side. But he had the weapon free at last. 'Beautifully preserved,' he said. 'As good as the day it was made.'

'What is it?'

'A PIAT—Projectile, Infantry, Anti-Tank. Early model but perfectly serviceable. It wouldn't dent a modern tank but it would smash any aircraft on earth to pieces.'

'I've done my national service like everybody else. I've seen something like that but

70

never fired one.'

'It's as simple as a rifle—simpler. Except that you put it on top of your shoulder instead of tucking the butt end under your armpit. The blast comes out of this nozzle.' Russell pointed. 'Don't let anyone stand behind you when you fire.' An unnecessary warning, he thought. If Mario ever came back here he'd come alone. 'And we'd better check that the projectiles still fire.' Russell picked one up and slipped it in.

'And the sighting?' Mario asked.

'Elementary. They're calibrated from open to a hundred and fifty yards, though with this early model a hundred and fifty would be a pretty desperate chance to go for.' Russell looked through the door at the strip of tarmac. 'Your plane won't be coming right up to this tower. Let's say it stops at sixty yards.'

He set the sights and looked through the door again. There was a cairn of stones beyond the strip where some peasant had once cleared his field. 'You see that heap of stones? Aim at it. It will take the projectile across the tarmac at about the right height for a kill on an aircraft. I take it that no local will hear us.'

'There are none now. That's why they use this particular airstrip.'

Russell handed the weapon to Mario de Var. 'Two pressures on the trigger,' he said. 'Good luck.'

Mario put the PIAT up, snuggling it till he had it comfortable. The weapon might be strange to him but Russell could see he was used to firearms. He took the first pressure and then the second.

The projectile went screaming away, invisible, and it smashed the cairn of stones into nothing.

'Good shot,' Russell said. 'And now we'll go.' A reaction from excitement had felled him but he gave clear and precise instruction to Mario. 'Use your handkerchief to clean that thing, then wrap it in what's left of the plastic and put it back. Close the lid and cover it up with rubble. Make it look as natural as you can. We'll go out backwards, smoothing our footmarks with the spade.'

In the car he fell into moody silence for he was going to do something distinctingly unmannerly: he was going to stand the de Vars up brutally. But the Baron had said that they wouldn't meet again. That had been in effect a dismissal. And as for Mario...

As for Mario, his nominal godson, he had left him a very handsome present, far better than any money he didn't need. The de Vars complained that they'd lost their estates but they still lived the life of medieval princes.

Charles Russell had decided to leave at once and the one thing he didn't want was fuss. If he shared his intention with Mario de Var— well, Mario was a well-bred man and it was probable that he wouldn't ask questions; but he would insist on seeing him off at the airport, and Russell was sick and tired of the Brethren. It was true that Mario wasn't one of them, an English mother and English schooling had made him inadmissible, but centuries of the Brotherhood's creed were still in his blood and undiminished. When he'd talked of the founding fathers to Russell he had made them sound like social workers. Charles Russell knew well they'd been no such thing; they'd been brutal and greedy and ruthlessly cruel. An occasional act of private piety was dust in the scale against organised evil. The American Brethren were no doubt worse with an empire built on addictive drugs, but it was a difference of degree not of kind.

Charles Russell felt a sudden revulsion against Sicily and all things Sicilian. He had an open ticket and there were two flights a day. The first class was very seldom full and if he didn't find a seat on the early flight he'd wait. He had a car at his disposal still. He had given Mario arms to fight drugs but he wanted no part of a feud between Brethren.

Mario de Var put him down at his hotel. 'Will you be swimming tomorrow?'

'Probably not.'

'Do you mind if I use the pool again?'

'Certainly.'

Mario made his adieux and drove away. Russell was glad that he hadn't had to lie a second time. He wouldn't be seeing his godson again and he hadn't wished to part on an untruth.

Somewhere in another place someone laughed.

4

Charles Russell spent a night at his club and in the morning took a stroll across the park to Queen Anne's Gate. Lord George received him warmly. 'You're looking well.'

'I'm feeling well. The change of interest did me good.'

'But you're back very early.'

'I was spending your money and I'd done all I could. When you spoke of a near-schism between the American Brethren and the mother stock in Sicily you were guilty of an understatement. They're clearly on a collision course. Your old-fashioned Sicilian Brother is still a criminal as he always was but he does have reservations about drugs. And he has more than reservations about the Americans flooding his country with them. Which is apparently what Loretto intends to do.'

'From which you deduce?'

'I do not deduce—there aren't the facts.'

'I stand corrected. Then what do you guess?'

'It occurs to me that if Loretto's next big target is Sicily it's unlikely to be England too.'

'Frank Loretto is here in London. Now.'

'Then bang goes my guess.'

'It doesn't follow.' Lord George was pleased to have caught Charles Russell in what was apparently a gross *non sequitur*.

'Why not?'

'Because he hasn't been anywhere near the drug people, which he would have if he'd been thinking of targetting us, and he hasn't done a thing which suggests an interest in the other rackets. Naturally the police have had him tailed. But he has done something entirely surprising.'

'Surprise me, then,' Charles Russell said.

'He's been down to your parts, Soken-le-Queen. Where that tip is which you told me about. He took photographs of the bridge and the island.'

'You must have had a damned good tail. The last mile of that road is open country.'

Lord George permitted an eyelid to flutter. 'A police helicopter just happened to be over-head. Come down to the box of tricks and I'll show you.'

He picked up the telephone and gave a brief order before they both went downstairs to the basement. A screen was already alight but blank, but as they sat down it came alive. A car had stopped at the mouth of the bridge and three men had got down and were taking photographs. One of them looked up at the helicopter and Lord George, who was holding a console, pressed a button. The picture stopped and froze as a close-up.

'That's Loretto,' Lord George said. 'Himself. Ugly little bastard, isn't he? And little is an important word. He's sensitive on the subject of size; he always wears built-up shoes and tries to walk long.'

'He's more than a little simian too. That long upper lip—'

'His grandmother was bog Irish, you know, the daughter of a New York patrolman. In

76

those days before they were both established the Italians married the Irish quite freely. They had a religion in common but not much else. Nowadays when they've got Cosa Nostra and a powerful lobby on top of that the Italians don't have to bed the Irish. Have you seen enough of Frank Loretto?'

'Plenty, thank you.'

Lord George flicked the button again and the film moved on. The three men ducked under the chain and crossed the bridge. They went to the fence round the tip. More photographs. Then they returned to the car and drove away. Lord George switched off and turned to Russell. 'And that concludes the entertainment.'

'Who were the other two men?' Russell asked.

'The thickset one is his personal bodyguard, something quite in the boss-gangster tradition. The other man is called John Aldo and is a very different cup indeed. He's almost an Old American and he's Frank Loretto's one-man think tank. He's cleverer than Loretto and subtler, and as a top Brother's right-hand man he's something new. Come upstairs again, we need to talk.'

Russell followed him but with private misgivings. Several questions had not yet been asked and to most of them he'd be obliged to give answers since those questions concerned the Executive's business. But what had happened at that airstrip was not. That had been Russell's private decision and one day he might live to regret it. In any case he wouldn't speak of it now.

Lord George sent for coffee and over it said: 'You've a remarkable nose for smelling the wind. This story about Loretto flooding Sicily with hard drugs. I take it you got that from your old friend the Baron.'

'I talked to the Baron for part of a luncheon but he's much frailer than I expected to find him. He's good for about half an hour, then he simply fades away into nothing. I got what I did from his son who's called Mario. He's also my godson, as you know, though not in religion.'

'And whose father is head of the Brethren in Sicily. Titular head since he's past any action, but I gather the job is more or less hereditary.'

'Mario will not inherit it. But he thinks like a Brother and in the pinches would act like one. Despite the English gloss on him he's still the quintessential Sicilian.'

'Sicilians,' Lord George said and left it. The tone had been less of contempt than of despair.

Charles Russell understood him at once for Lord George had a northern Italian wife. The normal form for a man like Lord George was Eton, the Brigade of Guards, and afterwards a merchant bank. Lord George had had the first but not the rest. Nor had he wanted them. As a youngest son he'd had a small allowance and on it had gone to Italy to paint. Professionally since he despised all amateurs and was ambitious to succeed as a painter. He had begun to sell in a difficult market when he'd met and married a Milanese heiress. She too had been ambitious but not to paint. She had insisted on return to England where her money had set up Lord George in politics. More important on this particular morning was the fact that she'd been a northern Italian. Sicilians would be barely human and Lord George, a good husband, would not have gainsaid her.

For the moment he was sitting in silence and Russell used it to think of Sicilians himself. They were clannish and corrupt and violent but what else would you expect them to be? Their island stood in western Europe but the blood of a dozen races ran in their veins—Norman, Frankish, Greek and Arabs, Moorish pirate and Spanish grandee. Their habit of mind was more Levantine than Latin.

Which made them unpredictable and to a

man like Russell the more interesting for it. What would Mario do when he had to choose?

Russell put the thought firmly behind him. All that was in the future and this was now. He was sitting in the Security Executive and there was unfinished business still on the table. Lord George had his eyes shut and Russell said sharply: 'Wake up, George. We're still at business.'

'My apologies. A foolish late night.'

'Your last remark was to say: "Sicilians." As a people I find them entirely fascinating but we're interested in a single Sicilian. Frank Loretto. Now what was he doing at Soken-le-Queen?'

Lord George was now awake and himself again. 'It doesn't make sense,' he said.

'It does not.'

'So consider it first from the point of *scale*. Somebody's tipping waste illegally. Some factory dumps its acrylonitryl—'

'Would that poison birds?'

'I gather it would poison anyone if he happened to eat food which it had touched. So some factory dumps a load at that tip instead of taking it to the appropriate place and paying to have it dealt with properly. It saves itself money but how much money? Wages and wear and tear on a lorry. The cost of treatment.

80

Three or four hundred pounds at most. That's quite below Frank Loretto's notice even if it were organised up into something to cover the whole of the country.'

'So where do we go from here?'

'We don't—you do. I'd like you to go back to Soken-le-Queen. I told you you had a marvellous nose and you admitted that new interest lifted you.'

And not a bad idea, Russell thought. He had said nothing to Lord George of Captain Cole but if anything had happened at Queens while he himself had been in Sicily that eccentric but observant seaman would certainly have noticed it. But if he went to Queens again he would go there with an open brief.

'What was the name of that toxic waste?'

'Acrylonitryl?'

'Yes, that was it. It may be we'll find more of it but there's a chance we're in the shadow of something else.'

'Such as what?'

Charles Russell told him. 'It's only a guess, mind.'

Lord George was silent for a considerable time; finally he said unhappily: 'If you said that to my wife she'd cross herself.'

The tanker had Belgian number plates but had

driven up to the Hook and rolled on there. Now it was rolling off at Parkeston Quay. Its manifest was in perfect order, a cargo of harmless agricultural pesticide. There were ecologists who said it was far from harmless but lately they'd been overplaying their hand and this particular chemical was still allowed in. The tanker went through Customs without fuss for it was a regular route and a common load. But two things about it were most uncommon: the first that the crew were three not two. That had been visible. But the other irregularity had not. For hidden in the driver's cab were explosives, detonators, and a machine-pistol, loaded.

The tanker began its journey to Soken-le-Queen. The road snaked and twisted, skirting the estuaries. It was impossible to make up time on it and the leader looked at his watch uneasily. The ship had been half an hour late in docking and he was working to a very tight timetable. He had to reach the tip and break his way into it; he had to dump his load and get back to Parkeston. And all in time to catch the same ship's return. He didn't dare to be caught in England, not after emptying his tank at Queens. How good were their defences and how quick? That was what he had been sent to find out.

He fussed and fretted as the tanker ground its way through the bends. There was more traffic than he'd been told to expect, and by the time he reached Queens the lost half-hour had increased to three-quarters. It was going to be a close-run thing.

In Soken-le-Queen they turned right for the jetty, putting on speed on the deserted road. They made a good deal of noise and Mathew Cole heard them. He got up, took a look, and on an instinct hid himself. He had seen trucks before but never a tanker.

It stopped at the mouth of the bridge and three men got out. One had the pistol on a sling around his neck and Mathew Cole blessed the instinct to hide. A second went up to the chain which barred the bridge, wrapping part of it in what looked like a bandage. He came back to the tanker and a wire trailed behind him. All three men knelt in the tanker's cover.

There was the unmistakable crack of a high explosive and the broken chain fell down in two pieces. The three men remounted the lorry and drove across the bridge.

Cole could do nothing but listen and he did. There was another crack as the padlock on the fence went, then the steady hum of the tanker's pump.

Presently the tanker returned. It had been too big to turn on the pad used by lorries and it backed across the narrow bridge awkwardly, one of the three men calling directions. Twice it struck the side girders but they held.

Once on the mainland it cumbrously turned. It took it four shunts to do it but it turned. The man with the pistol was still patrolling.

Unexpectedly he opened fire. The burst was several yards wide of Cole, who had been kneeling but now dropped flat. A furious voice came out of the tanker's cab.

'What in hell do you think you're playing at?'

'I saw something move.'

'What if you did? If they'd been able to stop us they'd have done so long ago.'

'Just the same...' The man with the pistol started to move again. He was heading straight at Mathew Cole.

'We're late already. Stop playing at television and come back.'

It had the unmistakable ring of authority and the gunman turned.

'And pick up those cartridge cases. All of them.'

He collected them and climbed back into the cab. The driver had the engine running and the tanker began to rumble up the road.

When its noise had finally faded Cole got up. He had been under fire before in war but never from a man he could see.

Charles Russell spent a day in inaction. He realised he was being used, exploited if you preferred the harsher word, but felt no resentment against Lord George: in Lord George's shoes he'd have done the same. He was living conveniently close to Queens and that was that.

Where something very unusual was happening—Charles Russell hadn't a doubt of that. He had interviewed and been interviewed many times, and he knew that when it came to judgement what mattered was not what had been said but what had not. His last talk with Lord George had been a classic example. Lord George had talked of Russell's marvellous nose, the old warhorse scenting the smoke of battle, but you didn't disturb the old horse in his paddock unless there was something real to smell. Lord George had given no hint of that and again Charles Russell felt no resentment. The rule of the Need to Know was sacrosanct and he was no longer in the Security Executive. Moreover if you gave a hint, a hint of what was there for the finding, it was as likely as not that you'd get the hint back confirmed. That was poor technique when you yourself were uncertain.

Instinct and experience both told Charles Russell that Lord George knew something he hadn't uttered, and he'd used the word 'acrylonitryl' which was hardly part of his normal vocabulary. So information had been coming across his desk, not enough to press the appropriate buttons but enough to set the alarm bells clanging.

And to an official skilled in the ways of others another incident in that interview had been odd. Charles Russell had named what was wholly unnameable and all Lord George had done had been to talk of his wife. That had been a deliberate duck. But duck from what? Experience suggested strongly that it had been a duck from what he suggested himself.

In which case Lord George would be not only uneasy but a very frightened man indeed.

When Charles Russell had reached these conclusions he telephoned. The number of Cole's prosperous boatyard had been registered in the Yellow Pages...Could he speak to Captain Mathew Cole? The Captain was unfortunately out. Could they help? No, thank you. He would ring again.

Russell put the telephone down. If Cole were out in the early evening Russell could make a good guess where he would be. He took out his car and drove to Soken-le-Queen.

Mathew Cole was on the bench by the jetty, his shotgun on the ground beside him. Russell noticed it and said politely: 'I hope you haven't had to shoot much.'

'Fortunately not.' Cole had a line to deliver and timed it carefully. 'But I've been shot at myself.'

'Have you indeed. Care to tell me the story?'

Cole told it matter-of-factly and Russell heard him in silence to the end. When Cole had finished he asked several questions.

'You say these men were Flemings. How do you know?'

'I can't speak Flemish but I know a few words of it.' Cole seemed to feel some explanation was necessary. 'When I was sailing out of Wivenhoe we went across to Belgium quite often. Often enough to be sure when it's spoken.'

'What have you done?'

'I've told the police—I felt I had to. Englishmen with lorries is one thing but foreigners with tankers is too much. But I kept quiet about the shooting.'

'Wisely.'

'They'd taken away the cases, you see. I'd be just another dim-witted old seaman, a man who shot seagulls and told tall tales. It would have discredited the rest of the story.'

'And what's happened since?'

'Two men came in a Council van and replaced the chain and the padlock on the fence inside. A helicopter came over too, the second in a week as it happens. It made several passes across the tip.'

'Did you notice its markings?'

'There were letters and numbers but no insignia.'

'Not Navy or Air Force?'

'None that I saw.'

Curious, Russell thought, but explicable. The police would have passed on the news of that tanker and some Department had taken precautionary action. 'And what are you going to do now?' he asked.

'I don't think I need to come back here. With a new chain and padlock the local cowboys won't get in, and whatever that tanker dumped it doesn't kill birds. I haven't seen a sick seagull for days. Besides, it's time I went back to work. As it happens I've had a very good charter.'

'Tell me,' Russell said. It had been spoken quite idly but struck immediate oil.

'I'm to take three men up the coast to the estuaries. It isn't normal cruising water but

Americans do the strangest things and the money is very good indeed.'

Charles Russell suppressed a rising excitement. 'Americans?' he asked. 'Three Americans?'

'So I was told. I only met one who'd come down from London. He said he'd been given my name by an agency. His own name was Aldo but he didn't mention the others. He gave me half the charter in cash.'

'Have you told the police of this?'

'Why should I?'

'I'm very glad indeed you haven't but also very glad you told me.' Russell hesitated but he'd have to tell more if he expected Mathew Cole to co-operate; finally, with deliberate formality: 'If those men are whom I suspect they are they're of the greatest interest to very senior people.'

Mathew Cole looked at Russell thoughtfully. 'You have the air, sir, of having been one yourself. Was it the secret service?'

'It was not. You may take one thing in this life for certain. If a man tells you he's been in the secret service you may be sure that that man is also a liar. I had nothing to do with MI5 or MI6: on the contrary our interests sometimes clashed. But I *was* in something they called Security. Security with quite a big capital.'

'And you want me to help?'

'I can only request it.'

Cole was looking unhappily doubtful. 'I have only this shotgun and I'm no longer young.'

'I can reassure you on that. Violence is something I want to avoid not provoke. This isn't going to be something for the box. But I'd like to put a bug on your ship just in case they say something which gives us a clue, and I'd like to put a trained man on board too.'

'What for?'

'Frankly, to see what you might miss. So a well-mannered young man will call at your boatyard and ask to be taken as a hand. He'll be qualified to serve as one too. It wouldn't do to send a lubber.'

Captain Mathew Cole thought this over carefully. Like all sailors he liked to be sure of his water. 'These three men are really dangerous? I mean dangerous to what really matters?'

'We sincerely fear so.' The 'we' had slipped out but he couldn't withdraw it.

Mathew Cole asked bluntly: 'Then why don't you nobble them?' He added without a hint of irony: 'I've heard that things like that sometimes happen.'

'Because it would be premature. I won't pretend that in the world of Security human life is always regarded as sacred but we're not yet sure what these men are planning.'

'And this trip of theirs might give you a clue?'

'There's a very good chance indeed,' Russell said.

'Then I'll do it.'

Charles Russell went home and rang Lord George.

5

His housekeeper was cooking his lunch so when the doorbell rang at noon next morning Charles Russell went to answer it himself. He opened to his neighbour above him, whom he liked. They were on excellent good-neighbourly terms for she was a widow and content to remain so. She never gave him that look he detested...Hm. No longer a boy but his head's all right. Very much all right. Handsome in a soldierly way and evidently in comfortable circumstances. I wonder...

Such reflections were in fact misplaced but Russell could read them and thought them impertinent. But with this neighbour he needn't watch for entanglements.

'What can I do this morning, madam? Is it eggs or a bottle of milk or sugar?' These were what she normally borrowed for she lived alone and was somewhat forgetful.

'I'm afraid it's a bit more unusual than that.'

'Then please come in.'

He gave her a chair and a glass of sherry.

'There's a bird in my kitchen,' she said. 'And it won't fly away.'

'Not a sick seagull.' Russell's heart had sunk since he'd have to wring its neck.

'It isn't a seagull, I think it's a pigeon. But not like the pigeons you see in the garden. It's smaller and it looks a lot wirier.'

'The window is open?'

'Of course it is.'

'What happens when you hoosh at it?' He was making the gesture of flapping a towel.

'It gets up from wherever it's sitting and flies round the room. But it won't go anywhere near the window. Then it settles again and it isn't house-trained.'

'May I come up and look?'

'Please do.'

She led him to her kitchen and he looked round. It was certainly not his idea of a kitchen. His own housekeeper's was always spotless but unmistakably a workshop for cooking. Here there wasn't a pot nor pan in sight. Presumably

92

they were in those elaborate cupboards whose doors bore formal swags and mouldings. There was an alcove with chair and table for eating. The whole thing had come from some woman's glossy and had been ordered as a single unit.

The bird was roosting on the electric cooker. It didn't seem distressed or sick and it looked at them with bright, curious eyes.

'It's a racing pigeon,' Russell said. 'A homer. It's a big sport in the north. They take them away in baskets, hundreds of miles, then let them loose. The first one home wins a lot of money.' There was a broad ring on the bird's left leg. 'Have you a magnifying glass?'

She brought one and he picked up the bird. It seemed perfectly used to being handled. Using the glass Russell read out the legend. *George Sidebottom. Bacup. Lancs.* 'Mr Sidebottom will be much distressed. He has probably lost a substantial bet and the bird itself is worth good money. I think it has lost its sense of direction. I've read that that sometimes happens but not why.'

'Then what do we do?'

'Ask someone who knows about birds. May I use your telephone?'

'Of course. There's an extension in the bedroom and if you don't mind I'll listen in.'

There was no RSPB in the directory but there was a number for the RSPCA. Russell rang it and a polite voice answered.

Yes, it was certainly a racing pigeon and almost certainly it had lost its compass. That could happen for a number of reasons. For instance, had there been thunderstorms recently?

Charles Russell said that he hadn't heard any.

Or any change in a field of magnetism?

How should he know? And what should they do?

Well, the one thing not to do was to put it out forcibly. If they did it wouldn't fly till it was ready and meanwhile local birds would attack it. Crows in particular.

So suppose they kept it, how did they feed it?

Birdseed if they could get it, or rice. But it had to be pudding rice, not the long grain. And plenty of water was important too.

Russell thanked him and rang off.

His neighbour returned from the bedroom indignantly. 'Pudding rice,' she said. 'Of all things! I don't have any pudding rice, far less the birdseed.'

'I'm going up to the town this morning. There's a pet shop and I'll try to get both.'

'That's very kind. I haven't the heart to put

94

it out—not to get pecked to death by other birds. But it does make the most disgusting messes. I hope it gets its navigation back soon.'

In the event the bird stayed only a few hours. For when he'd finished his conversation with Russell the man at the RSPCA had promptly made a call himself. He'd had a confidential circular about pigeons which lost their sense of direction. Any such cases should be reported urgently—most urgently. A telephone number followed the instruction and the man at the RSPCA had been sufficiently curious to check it. It had been a number at the Ministry of Defence.

Russell's neighbour was back at five o'clock and this time in a visible distress; she said without preamble: 'Colonel, there's a man at my flat and he says he's a policeman. He's got a basket and he says he wants that bird.'

'Have you let him in?'

'Not yet.'

'Then if I may I'll come up again.'

A man was standing outside the door and Russell gave him a quick, experienced look. He looked more like a middle-grade civil servant than a policeman but his warrant card, which he produced on demand, described him as an Inspector of Ministry of Defence Police.

Russell nodded and his neighbour opened the door. The Inspector didn't sit until asked to. Russell gave him good marks and asked: 'I understand you want that pigeon. You'll have to agree that's a little unusual. The MoD and a homing pigeon...' Russell left it at that and awaited an answer

'Very unusual indeed, sir, but there it is. If you care to ring the Ministry I can give you a number.' He produced a sheet of Ministry paper with a telephone number printed below it. Though Russell had no means of knowing it, it was the same number the Royal Society had. He went to the window and looked down on the gravel below. On it was an official-looking car with a driver.

If this was a trick it was very well organised. Moreover, what trick could it possibly be? The story was too tall for a con man and what con man would go to this trouble for a bird? But a lifetime had taught Charles Russell caution and he returned to his chair and asked the Inspector: 'Suppose we decline to hand it over?'

'That would be unfortunate, sir, since it would mean a delay. But there is power in the Act'—he quoted one by name and number—'to take the bird without your permission.'

'You mean you could just seize it here and now?'

'Oh, no. I should have to get a warrant but I could.'

Charles Russell looked at his neighbour thoughtfully. Women were much better than men at asking the really awkward questions. The lady obliged.

'Why do you want that bird at all?'

'I'm afraid I cannot tell you that. But I'm authorised to say that it's a matter of Security.'

'Security,' she said contemptuously. She was a reader of the Sunday *Observer* and she made it sound like a dirty word. 'What are you going to do with it?'

He hesitated, but finally told her. 'It will be rushed to a laboratory, madam.'

'Nothing to do with vivisection?'

'Certainly not.' He was clearly offended. 'It will be examined, fed and watered and cared for. When it's ready to fly it will fly quite freely.'

His neighbour looked back at Russell who nodded. They went into the kitchen together and the Inspector took his basket with him. The pigeon had eaten some rice but not the seed. When the Inspector took the lid off the wickerwork the pigeon didn't need to be handled; it hopped happily into the basket and settled. Evidently it was used to baskets.

'Thank you, madam, and thank you, sir.'

Now that he had the bird the Inspector relaxed. 'If you'd obliged me to get a warrant it would have cost time. Time,' he added, 'which we cannot afford.'

They heard the official car drive away. It seemed to be driven rather harder than usual.

Russell's neighbour cleaned up the last of the droppings. 'And what do you make of that?' she asked.

'He was genuine and it was something important.'

'Nothing more specific than that?'

'I can't be sure.'

He bid her good evening and went back to his flat. It was perfectly true that he couldn't guess, but birds, he was thinking—it was very unusual, quite without precedent. He'd had little to do with birds before beyond feeding them in the worst of the weather but now they seemed to be everywhere, as ubiquitous as Frank Loretto. First that sick seagull which had led him to Soken-le-Queen and Captain Cole; and now a homing pigeon which had apparently lost its power to navigate. No doubt it could all be explained by coincidence but that wasn't a word in Charles Russell's vocabulary.

6

Next morning Charles Russell was reading his newspaper when the telephone interrupted him. He picked it up and a familiar voice said: 'Charles?'

'Good morning, George. What mischief is it now?' It was a measure below his normal urbanity but Russell was a little annoyed. He was being used which he didn't object to, but he was also being kept in the dark and that he was inclined to resent. He had telephoned to Lord George when he'd last left Queens and given him Mathew Cole's latest news. Lord George had thanked him gratefully but hadn't rung back. At the lowest it was rather casual.

But Lord George's next remark was mollifying. 'I owe you an apology but I can't say why on an open line. Instead I'm sending you Doctor Molly Grant. You've heard of her, of course.'

'The name rings a faint bell.'

'It should ring one much louder. Most Departments have their own tame scientist who will stubbornly fight that Department's

99

corner but Molly Grant is above all that. She goes in and out of Number Ten at will. She also gets well paid to do so. She has some sort of official title as well but it doesn't change what she does in fact. She can take a broad view and the Prime Minister trusts her.'

'What's her line?'

'Formally she's a nuclear physicist but she isn't interested in the big bangs. Nor even in what happens afterwards, the wretches who haven't been granted quick death but are going to die. But she's the world's Number One on radiation in very small quantities. It's called micro-radio-activity and since everything, nowadays, must have initials its name in the trade is MCRA.'

'What's she like?'

'Not at all one's idea of a woman scientist. In passing can you give her lunch?'

'Gladly.'

'Then make it a good one. She's fond of food though she doesn't show it. Also, I hear reliably, of men. Not at all the bluestocking battle-axe.'

'She sounds interesting—I wish I knew more of her. I've got the usual books or could reach them but they only give you the formal facts.'

'I'd thought about that and I'll send you a brief. She's on her way by car already but a dispatch rider will beat her easily. She'll be with you about half-past twelve but the brief will be in your hands by noon. You won't find it what you expect at all. And in passing a word of fraternal warning. Don't mention the Royals.'

'I wasn't going to but why shouldn't I?'

'Every alpha plus brain is allowed an eccentricity and hers is that she's a lunatic Jacobite. She recently declined an honour—perfectly logically from her point of view. All honours traditionally spring from the Crown, and to Doctor Molly Grant and her kind the Crown is some obscure foreign nobleman. They even put special stamps on their letters?'

'And what does Her Majesty's Mail make of that?'

'It doesn't seem to care a damn so long as there's a proper one too.'

All this was said in amusement, not outrage, and Russell smiled. Lord George came of a great Whig house and he wouldn't be over-impressed by thrones.

'But in every other way she's quite normal and of course she has a great deal to tell you. And now I must arrange that DR.'

Who arrived on time on a Japanese motorcyle. Russell signed for the parcel and began to read the brief.

101

As Lord George had said it would, it surprised him. This wasn't the history of some clever nobody fighting her way through the jungle of Science to achieve in the end a rather dull recognition. Molly Grant had progressed with the cool panache granted only to the genuinely outstanding. Her parents had been comfortably off and had sent her to a fashionable girl's school—fashionable but not famous for academic achievement. But one of the mistresses had been exceptional and Miss Grant had won a scholarship smoothly. At Cambridge she had read Mathematics and her First had seemed (but hadn't been) effortless. She'd been at home in that astonishing world where men talked happily of numbers greater than infinity.

After that two years at a Dutch university where mathematics had slipped easily into nuclear physics. Then a researcher at Yale where she'd published two papers, two controversial papers which had stood the world of physicists on its head. Back to Cambridge as a junior fellow, then a year as a Department's tame cat. Now she had the ear of Number Ten. She never talked down to laymen—never; but she had the gift of making them understand.

When Russell heard a car on the gravel he went out to it to greet his guest. The driver was holding the door for his passenger and what emerged first was a pair of elegant legs. The shoes had sensible heels but had clearly cost money. The rest of the woman followed lithely, ignoring the driver's courteous arm. She was taller than average and dressed for London. She wore a hat, a small affair like a turban, and black gloves. Her face was handsome rather than formally beautiful. Russell guessed her age at the early forties.

'Doctor Molly Grant?'

'Just Molly Grant.'

'Then please come in.'

He settled her in a chair and asked. 'A gin drink or a glass of sherry?'

'Sherry, please. George tells me you're an expert on sherry.'

'Lord George has got it wrong for once. I'm very far from being an expert but I do keep a very drinkable sherry.' He was feeling at ease with this eminent woman who so clearly wore her honours lightly. As he poured he explained. 'I was in Spain for a very short time in the war (where hadn't he been in the war? he wondered) and came in contact with one of the great sherry families. I was able to do them a modest service which they've repaid by sending me sherry ever since.'

She drank a mouthful of the wine and said: 'This is good.'

'If you like it it's good. If you don't it's nothing.'

She gave him an approving look. 'Exactly how I feel myself. Expertise on wine can be terribly boring.'

She had finished her sherry and Russell went to the sideboard. When he returned she had taken her hat off. Her hair was black and cut in a cunning bell. She had also taken off one glove. She saw his enquiring look and said: 'I had an accident once and it isn't pretty.'

'I'm sorry.'

'You shouldn't be—it was all my own fault. When you play with the sort of toys that I do you're a fool if you take a chance. I did. So I always keep a glove on even in bed. That is, unless I'm in bed alone, a situation I regard as unnatural.'

He laughed as he could see he was meant to. They had established an immediate sympathy, less that of a still-active man and a woman who was delighted to be one than the stronger bond of common tastes and habits of mind which meshed neatly together.

'You'll stay to lunch, of course?'

'That's very kind.'

She was too well-mannered to talk business at table but chatted easily of trifles of interest. She had heard that he no longer played eighteen

104

holes so how did he keep his still-admirable figure?

He watched the carbohydrates carefully and twice a week he took a swim. Might he venture to use the same adjective and question?

She was evidently pleased and answered gladly. She had never been any good at games so she went to a gymnasium regularly. Well, not quite the usual smelly gymnasium and it wasn't a karate club either, where women weren't as a rule very welcome. It had been started in one of the mugging scares by two sergeants from the Physical Training Corps. It was for women only and flourishing mightily. Officially it was for self-defence only, how to deal with a rapist or a man after your bag, but if you wanted to learn the real rough stuff they'd teach you. Unarmed combat: it was excellent exercise. But it had led her into a little contretemps.

Really?

Indeed. As it had happened she'd been mugged herself. The man had gone for her bag but she'd grabbed his hand first. She had given him a Glasgow handshake. He hadn't rolled and had dislocated his shoulder. Thereafter it had been a bit of a mess.

'Where was the mess in that? It was self-defence.'

'The trouble was that the man was black. If

he'd been white there'd have been only formalities but the fact he was black brought in You Know Who. Finally I was formally charged.'

'With what?'

'Causing grievous bodily harm. Apparently I'd overdone it. I should have punched his nose or kicked his shins. But it was a tabloid which really set the affair on fire. There's nothing against your running a headline saying *Eminent Woman Scientist Roughs Up Mugger* but you're breaking the law or held to be breaking it if you say *Eminent Woman Scientist Roughs Up Black Mugger.* So what they did, and they made a lot of it, was to print the headline without the adjective but under it, in a different column, the photograph of a villainous-looking black in a hospital bed.'

'Naughty,' Russell said. 'What happened then?'

'I had one piece of luck. The mugging had been in Oxford Street so I went first before a tough old Stipendiary. If it had been some milk-fed bench of beaks, the sort which goes on courses where they teach them about their social duties—if that bench had been thinking progressive thoughts it would have sent me down or even up and then I'd have been in serious trouble.'

'So what happened with the Stipendiary?'

'The Stipendiary didn't like it at all and he was very, very, very careful. He hardly mentioned the law, nothing which could have been taken to a Divisional Court, but simply found, as a matter of fact, that on the evidence I'd done nothing excessive.'

'You were lucky,' Russell said. 'When that lot gets after you it can pull many strings.'

'I know.'

There were coffee and brandy set out in the living-room. Freed from the restraints of table-talk Molly Grant came straight to business. 'Have you heard of micro-radio-activity?'

'I heard of it for the first time this morning. Lord George said you were the leading pundit.'

'Unfortunately I'm no such thing. We know it exists but not all that it does, especially over the years—long term.' She asked unexpectedly: 'Do you wear a luminous wristwatch?'

'No.'

'Or have you had an X-ray recently?'

'I had one a couple of years ago on a leg.'

'Then you're almost certainly MCRA. An ordinary Geiger would show you clean but super-sensitive instruments would read. We keep them in a laboratory in Somerset. The front of the place is a furniture factory but behind it is the small space we need. The thing is so secret it doesn't exist.'

'So you're taking this MCRA pretty seriously.'

'We're obliged to. Look what's happening near any nuclear power station. Of course, it's only a linear relationship—'

'I've heard the term but I'm not sure what it means.'

'Two lines on a graph not directly related but looking much the same in pattern. In this case one line is proximity to a nuclear power station and the other the incidence of leukemia in children.'

'That gets into the papers from time to time. It's usually blamed on a hushed-up leakage.'

'We're perfectly content it should be. If somebody got ideas about MCRA there'd be a scare to make all others look silly. And we suspect that miniscule doses of radiation do curious things to navigating animals.' She took out a silver cigarette case. 'I shouldn't be doing this,' she said. 'There's a linear relationship here too, this time between lung cancer and smoking. There's no clinical proof which would go down in a court but the two curves frighten me. I tried to give up but put on weight and got irritable so I've cut it down to a dozen a day.' She looked at the cigarette case and added: 'But I'm well within my ration for the day.'

He lit her cigarette and asked: 'Then may I smoke a cigar?'

'By all means. Why not?'

'Some women say it spoils the curtains.'

'And so it does. But they're not my curtains.'

She could be blunt when she wished and Charles Russell approved it. 'You were talking of navigational animals.'

'A year or two ago, on the Malabar coast, a school of porpoises was washed up on the beach. They were alive and apparently perfectly well except that they had lost their way. There was a nuclear power station some miles up the coast. A coincidence and I've been trained to dislike them?'

'What happened to the porpoises?'

'If they'd been left alone they'd have recovered and gone back to sea. But the locals had never seen a porpoise; they thought they were some sort of sea devil. Being high-caste Hindus they couldn't kill them so they sent for their low-caste neighbours who did. They walked down the lines with spears, impaling them.' She made the gesture of striking down vertically. 'The beasts must have taken a long time to die. Charming people, Indians, aren't they?'

'Some of them are extremely nasty.' Charles

Russell had been thinking fast. 'And that bird?' he enquired. 'My neighbour's pigeon.'

'It had a measurable dose of MCRA. I was coming to that in good time.'

'I beg your pardon.'

'Then let's start with events at Soken-le-Queen. Captain Cole reports an illegal dumping and the Council sends round a man to make repairs. But when you reported a foreign tanker it began to make no sense at all. Or at any rate not for industrial waste. A local firm with PCBs on its hands can save a few pounds by tipping at Queens instead of sending it where it should rightly go; but to send toxic waste by sea from the Continent would cost more than having it properly treated. Much more. Prima facie therefore that tanker's load was something other than toxic waste.'

'If you're trying to make my flesh creep you have.'

'I can tell you Number Ten was scared stiff. If that tanker's load had been what we feared we should have had to clear a large part of East Anglia, including you from this very enviable flat. There would have been national and understandable panic. But it wasn't what we feared or not yet.'

'And then?'

'Then there was the affair of that pigeon. In

the laboratory it was faintly positive. In passing it has now flown away happily.'

'So you think that tip was once infinitesimally active? Like me after that X-ray, or that bird?'

'We know it was. We brought our instruments down from darkest Somerset and put them over the tip in a chopper.'

Russell had been fascinated but not convinced. 'But the financial aspect again,' he said. 'Would it have been worth anyone's while to bring over a load of low grade RA spoil?'

'Definitely—if done as a trial run. To test how soon we'd latch on to the big stuff. If they really intend to push that onto us it won't be in proper and safe containers. Nothing like BNF in Britain. They cost the earth and would leave no profit. But it will have to be sufficiently masked to get it through Belgium and over the sea before it goes up in our faces here, and merely masked it would also be detectable. No thanks to us the trial *was* detected. Thanks instead to that God-given pigeon. But *they* don't know about the pigeon; they will be thinking that the trial run succeeded. And if they are thinking that they'll go ahead. With the dangerously hot stuff. When we're in appalling, quite unthinkable trouble.'

'Is that the current theory, then?'

'I rather prefer the word "hypothesis"—it's the only thing we have to work on. But we ought to know for sure tomorrow. If the Executive's arrangements are as efficient as usual Captain Cole is now at sea with Loretto. On a ship with a bug and a trained observer. What he says and does are going to be interesting.'

'I confess I'm curious.'

'You needn't be. There's a meeting at Number Ten tomorrow—the PM, myself and, of course, Lord George. The PM asked me to invite you too.'

'But what can I offer?'

'Experience and your beautiful eyes. And you happen to live right on top of the action.'

'I'm flattered.'

'I can't think why. So at noon precisely at Number Ten, and a car will be sent to pick you up.'

The three men had left their car at the boatyard for they would need it again to drive on to Parkeston Quay. They had paid their hotel bill, leaving generous tips, and extra to the car-hire firm for collecting the car from where they would leave it. Frank Loretto who'd risen from petty crime and had never lost the instincts which went with it had suggested that they bilk both and run, but Aldo had dissuaded him from an evident foolishness. It was unlikely they'd ever return to England, but why risk the complication of writs if they did? To Frank Loretto, the head of the Brethren, the money concerned was barely noticeable. Privately Aldo was thinking contemptuously that these gutter children could never be changed.

Cole came out onto the hard to meet them and Aldo introduced the two others as 'my principal and his personal servant'. The cruiser was at her buoy in the creek. She was a considerable vessel which could sleep four comfortably with a foredeck which could take deckchairs and a generous well. They went out to her in a tender and climbed aboard. The hand had already started the engine.

They began to work out of the creek very slowly. Layton wasn't a modern marina on open sea but it was in reach of London and not yet expensive. Most of the boats they were carefully avoiding had some sort of motor as well as sail, since when the wind was wrong, as it mostly was, the creek was far too narrow for beating.

They cleared the creek into open sea and at a nod from Loretto, Cole spun the wheel to port. They were cruising up the coast going roughly north-east. Every quarter of a mile

113

or so the coast was cut by a creek or small estuary.

At the first of these Frank Loretto told Cole to stop. In fact this creek petered out at Soken-le-Queen, at Sheep's Island and the abandoned quay. Loretto turned to Captain Cole.

'How deep is that creek?'

'At high tide I'd put it at roughly three fathom.'

'How much is that?'

'Say eighteen feet.'

'And at low?'

'Very little.'

'Then please go on.'

They made three more stops at the mouths of small estuaries with the same and entirely fruitless exchanges till Captain Cole said politely: 'Sir. If deep water is what you're looking for there isn't any till Miller's Sound. That's almost the open sea and quite deep. There used to be a flourmill there and in the war it was used by at least one frigate.'

'Then let's have a look at Miller's Sound.'

John Aldo had taken a chart from a briefcase. 'Sixty-five feet at the mouth,' he said.

'The mouth won't do. We'll have to go up a bit.'

They went up half a mile and stopped again. Loretto asked Aldo: 'How much now?'

'No reading here.'

Loretto turned to Cole in enquiry. Cole smiled and said: 'I can soon find out.' He spoke to the hand in the well, who left it; he went up to the foredeck carrying a lead; he cast it and called the depth. 'Eight fathom. That's forty-eight feet.'

He went back to the well where he stowed the lead. The engine was idling and he started to tinker with it. There was nothing whatever wrong with the engine but he wanted to observe the three passengers. They were sitting in a row on a bench and now they were speaking in rapid dialect. The hand had some Italian or he wouldn't have been picked for the job but of this speech he could make nothing at all. But he noticed one thing which he reported as significant. Aldo had taken a second paper from his briefcase. The hand wasn't able to see it in detail but he was sure it was a photograph of a ship. They seemed to be comparing it with the chart and he caught the word 'Belinda' clearly.

Presently Frank Loretto stood up. 'Thank you, Captain. We'll go back now.'

They went back to the buoy where the tender was floating and Cole motored them back to the hard and dry land. John Aldo paid him the second half of the charter and all three men got into the waiting car. They drove to Parkeston Quay and the ferry and their tail slipped on board her smoothly behind them. At the Hook he almost lost them but didn't. He followed them to a hotel in Ostend.

7

When Loretto and his attendants had gone the Executive's man on Cole's cruiser acted fast. He went first to what looked like a post office van which had been parked on a side street in Layton town and had been taping what the bug had picked up. With it he drove to Queen Anne's Gate for he'd been told to report to Lord George in person.

...No, they hadn't seemed in the least suspicious, they'd been talking between themselves quite freely, and they had done two rather interesting things: they had sent him to take a sounding of the depth in Miller's Sound and they'd had a chart which they'd seemed to compare with a photograph. That photograph had looked like one of a ship. He had also caught the word 'Belinda'.

The operator had been thanked for his

services and had delivered the tape to Lord George directly.

Who began to run it but at once gave up. He had an Italian wife and fluent Italian but was defeated by this colloquial Sicilian. A nuisance. He'd have to send the tape to headquarters at Ealing and they didn't have a tame Sicilian. To arrange the translation might take several hours.

In the event it took the best part of the night but was very well done. The translator had kept his voice impersonal but he had managed to differentiate between Aldo's clear New England accent—even in Sicilian he had sounded like an educated man—and the Square State drone of Loretto. The Loretto voice had come in first:

'Forty-eight feet, the man said. That's pretty deep.'

'It looks to be high tide.'

'So what?'

John Aldo's cool voice said matter-of-factly: *'When it's low it's going to be less, you know.'*

'How much less?'

'I don't know. This is a big stretch of water. Say twelve feet.'

'Which leaves thirty-six feet.'

'I make it the same.' John Aldo was acid. *'Enough to hide Belinda?'*

'I can't be sure. The ship herself, I'm almost

certain, but we might have to cut off her masts to be safe.'

'And of any other ship with the hot stuff.'

'Or choose smaller ones.'

'Which wouldn't pay.'

Lord George poured a stiffish brandy and drank it. He then telephoned to the Prime Minister on the Executive's private line. 'Clement? Are you alone?' The use of the Christian name was ominous. Lord George was the Prime Minister's uncle-in-law and in social life it was 'George' and 'Clement'. But in business they were always punctilious: it was 'Prime Minister' and 'Lord George' as a matter of course.

'You sound excited.'

'I'm more than that. We've had the tape from that bug which we put on Cole's cruiser.'

'Well?'

'I think I'd better bring it over.'

'As bad as that?'

'A good deal worse.'

'Then you'd better bring it over at once. Before the meeting at noon. I want to be properly briefed before that.'

Lord George was shown up to what was called the morning room. He was carrying the recorder and turned it on. The Prime Minister listened and at the end went white. 'The last

118

bit again, if you please,' he said. 'The bit where they say "hot stuff" clearly.'

Lord George obliged and watched the Prime Minister. His colour was coming back but slowly. 'I seldom drink at this hour,' he said. 'But I need one. And you?'

'I've had one, thanks.'

And he did need that drink, Lord George was thinking. For now it wasn't some greedy industrialist's PCBs; it wasn't that MCRA which Molly Grant understood but few others. It was for real. Lord George's nephew had a tiny majority and he was Prime Minister of an unforgiving democracy whose east coast would soon be alive with nuclear waste. Uninhabitable.

The drink had done him good and he said: 'I've already asked Molly Grant to attend at twelve. And she's bringing Charles Russell. It's now half-past eleven so stick around.'

'Right.'

Lord George was not displeased; he had a card. A doubt had occurred to him and he'd spent all night on the telephone to America. For any suspect ship which came from Belgium would be lying in one of the dozen small harbours which ran northwards from Ostend to Holland; and the several Belgian nuclear power stations were all inland. So how did you get

119

their waste from site to sea? You couldn't load it on an ordinary lorry without leaving a trail of disaster behind you; some specialised transport was obviously necessary. What specialised transport? Well, that had been a scent and he'd followed it.

He was feeling a modest self-satisfaction. The talk at noon would be all of great issues, the awesome political implications; he might be asked to take action he almost certainly couldn't. But he wasn't going to appear empty-handed.

The car which collected Russell that morning had been large and slow but very well driven and it dropped him at Number Ten at five to twelve. He was shown upstairs and was privately glad of it. He had been in the Cabinet Room and admired it but had always found it overpowering. Molly Grant and Lord George had arrived already and Russell accepted coffee and sat down. They greeted one another but didn't talk. All of them knew they were there for great matters. The tension began to increase unbearably.

When the Prime Minister came in the two men rose and all three faces turned to him sharply. He was grey and drawn but entirely in control of himself. A brave and resilient man,

Russell thought. He wished them all good morning, then said:

'Lord George and I have the advantage of Doctor Molly and Russell. Both of us have heard this tape and you have not. It was picked up by a bug on a cabin cruiser in Essex, courtesy of a Captain Mathew Cole. I would like to do something for Captain Cole but I cannot see a way to contrive it. If he were a second-rate actor or civil servant I could arrange a CBE very easily.'

It was a pleasantry to relieve the tension. All three smiled politely but it had failed.

The Prime Minister ran the tape into silence, watching Charles Russell and Molly Grant. Charles Russell, who had seen crises before, was showing no sign of emotion whatever but the face of Doctor Molly Grant had frozen into the Greek mask of horror.

The Prime Minister said: 'It would be proper to give you five minutes to think. After that I'm afraid there will have to be questions.'

He gave them five minutes precisely, then looked first at Doctor Molly Grant. 'The first question is on the extent of the danger. How much high-risk atomic waste does Belgium hold?'

Molly Grant had used her five minutes to think. 'The country is awash with it, facing the

121

same problems as we are. What one of them called the hot stuff is remarkably like a vampire's body. Nobody wants it buried near them even with a stake through its heart. Propose a new site for safe disposal and the inhabitants are up in arms. The life of the local MP gets unbearable. And it's an appallingly expensive business.'

'So anyone with a short cut would make money?'

'He would indeed. You could count it in millions.'

'Do you think the Belgian government knows?'

She shrugged. 'That's not for me.'

The Prime Minister turned to Russell who answered. 'They wouldn't know officially. But it couldn't be done without their connivance.'

'So if we challenge them—?'

'There'll be indignant noises.'

The Prime Minister in turn took time to think; finally he said to Lord George: 'So there's enough in this to interest Loretto. The next question is a more practical one. Has he the organisation to handle it?'

'I think we must assume he has or he wouldn't have taken it on in the first place. Moreover there is other evidence. Doctor Grant

122

spoke of Belgium awash with nuclear waste. Unlike Holland it's not yet awash with drugs but there's a flourishing and expanding drug trade and most of that is controlled by Loretto. Leaving aside the low-grade pushers he'll have competent men at the higher levels. Also he's now in Ostend himself.'

'So where do we go from here?'

No one spoke.

'Colonel Russell?' It was a little sharp.

'If you're asking about the politics they look to me extremely bleak. If this were some unimportant stateling, I don't doubt Lord George could arrange some action. But Belgium isn't an unimportant stateling: she's a valuable ally in NATO.' It was spoken as an actor would speak it, knowing that the line was untrue. But in the existing climate it had to be said. It was a necessary genuflection, a priest bobbing as he crossed his altar. 'Lord George can send a man to Belgium, a man to sniff about for *Belinda*. It would at least be useful to know where she sails from. Thereafter the coastguards or maybe the Navy—'

'I don't like that.' It was the Prime Minister, deceptively emollient. 'To sink her would be an act of war. All either of those forces could do would be to escort her back into Belgian waters. Leaving her free to try again at a place

123

and time we do not know.' He looked at Lord George. 'Your opinion, please.'

'I've already got a man on *Matilda* but there may be another possible line.' They all looked at him but still in silence. 'We're agreed that the Belgian government will connive but it will barely risk open collaboration. Active atomic waste is dangerous, it is moved about in special vehicles. The Belgian government won't dare use its own so someone has got to move it from plant to the sea.'

'Good thinking,' the Prime Minister said. 'Good thinking' was in no way patronising. It was his shorthand that he wished to hear more.

Lord George produced a company's business card and passed it round.

La Compagnie Générale pour la Déchargement de Déchets et d'Effluents Industriels SA.

'It sounds even more pompous in English, I'm afraid. "Company General for the disposal of industrial wastes and effluents." But it's a perfectly respectable company. Its barges sail up and down the great rivers to the establishments which deal with it. It also has lorries to do the same thing.' Lord George asked a question of Molly Grant. 'Could those lorries be used to carry nuclear waste?'

She told him what she had told Charles Russell. 'It could be sufficiently masked to get it out to Miller's Sound and sunk there. But when the light masking broke down there'd be a major disaster, another Chernobyl.'

'So it wouldn't be properly packed for transport?'

'To do so would cut the profit to nothing. Loretto is in this affair for the money.'

The Prime Minister came in sharply again. 'I thought you said it was a respectable company.'

'It is, or rather it has been so far.'

'Well?'

'There is one thing about it I do not like.' Lord George was taking his time in the telling. He'd been up all night on his line to America, talking to professional colleagues several of whom were in his debt. He wasn't going to have his big scene upstaged.

'When heavy industry collapsed in south Belgium the Flemings in the north saw their chance. They are disciplined, hard-working and not over-Unionised. The Americans too saw an opening and took it. Now north Belgium is full of American-owned firms—almost strike free and prospering mightily. The *Compagnie Générale* is one of them. Fifty-one per

125

cent of its equity is held in America by what we should call a nominee.'

'Why don't you like that?'

Lord George delivered his punchline with aplomb. 'Because the nominee is owned by the Brethren.'

It took a second or two to sink in and the Prime Minister winced. When he had recovered he said: 'So they could force a special meeting at any time. They could get rid of the present Board at will.'

'If it didn't do what Loretto demanded—yes.'

'What do you know of the Board?'

'Their names.' Lord George began to read them out, but when he came to the third Molly Grant stopped him. 'Professor Julius van Eyck,' she said. 'I knew him at Leyden.'

'What sort of man is he?'

'He's a Nobel Prizewinner.'

'I meant his politics.'

'I told you—he's a Nobel Prizewinner.'

For the first time that morning there was the healing sound of genuine laughter. Nobody won a Nobel Prize unless their politics were acceptable to the liberal, dourly enlightened humanists who held it in their power to award it.

'So if he knows what we suspect he won't approve.'

126

'He emphatically will not. But *does* he know? He won't be an executive director; he'll be on that Board for name and fame.'

For a moment the atmosphere had almost tangibly lightened but the Prime Minister brought them back to reality. 'But he might suspect?'

'Indeed he might. He's nobody's fool.'

'How well do you know him?'

'Pretty well. He's an orthodox nuclear physicist—big bangs and all that—whereas I've wandered down a sidestreet of my own. But we still have interests in common; we correspond.'

'Would you be prepared to talk to him? If he's the sort of man he seems to be and if he does suspect what he wouldn't approve of—'

'He might bare his breast to another scientist? Just so.' Molly Grant looked at the Prime Minister, concealing a strong but private amusement. He was beating about the bush unnecessarily but he'd also been having a terrible morning. She said coolly: 'I'll leave tomorrow, then.'

'I'm very greatly obliged.' The Prime Minister began to sum up. 'So we've a man looking for a ship called *Belinda* and the chance of some information through Doctor Grant. It isn't a lot in a dangerous crisis.' He gave a half-look at Lord George who caught it.

'If you were thinking of something equally dangerous I'm afraid the Executive cannot help you. Men who will kill for money do exist. But not when you tell them that the target intended is a man called Frank Loretto. No.'

It had been a little too forthright for the Prime Minister's taste and he tried to cover embarrassment with a jest. 'So what we need is an old-fashioned assassin. Somebody with a private motive to kill.'

'They don't grow on trees.'

When Russell reached his flat that evening he was tired and cross. He had declined the offer of a car to drive him home—he didn't feel that he had earned the convenience—and the train had been delayed and crowded. As he let himself in his housekeeper met him. Normally she was unemotional but this evening she was clearly excited.

'There's a gentleman in the spare bedroom, sir.'

Charles Russell too was startled. 'What?'

'Some foreign name, sir. I didn't catch it.'

'Was it by any chance de Var?'

'Something like that. And he said he was your godson.'

'He is.'

'Also he seems to be pretty sick. It looks like some fever. I hope I did right to let him in.'

'Perfectly right.'

Charles Russell walked to the spare room briskly. Mario was on the bed, in pyjamas, his clothing strewn around the room. The heating had been turned on full but he was shivering under at least four blankets. He started to speak but Russell silenced him. 'Malaria?' he enquired.

Mario nodded. Officially malaria had been stamped out in Sicily but Russell had taken quinine when he'd gone there himself. There were other and newer drugs for malaria but Russell believed that quinine was still best.

He asked: 'Do you know what sort of malaria?'

'They tell me its benign tertian.'

'How long have you had this attack?'

'Two days and a bit.'

Russell had had BT himself. 'Then with any luck you'll be easier tomorrow. You've taken quinine, of course?'

'I have a drug.'

'Then I'll send you a glass of hot milk. Try to sleep. We'll talk tomorrow but just one question now. Why are you here?'

'I've come to kill Frank Loretto,' Mario said.

The story as Mario had told it next morning had had a nightmare's harsh and vivid reality. It had begun when he'd been talking to the youngest of his half-sisters. There were two others whom he thought rather dull, ladies who had married highly suitable husbands and were happy in their traditional trades of church, children and cooking. But this youngest sister's history had been different. She had had a hot admirer once but he hadn't been considered suitable. He was prosperous and of good reputation but he also happened to be an attorney and to the Baron de Var that had not been acceptable.

She hadn't been in love with him and when the inevitable had happened had bowed to it gracefully. She had taken her vows and become a nun. But her Order was neither enclosed nor severe, the food was edible and there was wine at meals. Holidays were allowed with parents and on these a habit need not be worn indoors. The good Sisters might even occasionally smoke provided this was done in private. There were impious cynics who said that this Order was no more than a rather comfortable club for spinster ladies of unimpeachable lineage but the cynics were not entirely right. It was a teaching Order and its standards were high. In status Enrica de Var was a religious but teaching had in turn taught her much and Mario was of the firm opinion that she knew more of the world than her two lay sisters. Also she had wit and a certain style, and since he needed family advice it was to her he had turned on a question of conscience.

He told her of the American Brethren's plans to flood their native island with hard drugs. She agreed at once that this was intolerable, and slowly, very slowly indeed, he began to lay the cards down one by one...He knew how the drugs came in and he knew when the next consignment was due. It was just possible that he had means to stop it but that action would involve crude violence.

Then would lives be lost?

Very certainly they would.

The lives of drug smugglers?

And of those who would later push them on the streets.

Her reaction to this had not disappointed him. She hadn't indulged the tedious cliché that two wrongs could never make a right nor

131

recommended him to the family priest whom he knew she regarded as a half-educated peasant. Her approach had been more subtle; she had asked: 'Whatever you mean to do you will do alone?'

'I must.'

'You won't be leading others into a crime?'

He shook his head.

'Then I was born a de Var just as much as you were.'

He had understood her perfectly. She was a religious but a patrician too. The de Vars had been fiercely Catholic for centuries and she herself had taken formal vows. She couldn't and wouldn't approve a crime but she knew that in her brother's eyes this wouldn't be a crime at all. She left morals behind her and asked practical questions.

'It sounds very long odds against you, brother.'

'I'm not going to take them on in a gunfight. I cannot tell you how or where but I've a more powerful weapon than pistols or bombs.'

She let it go with a cool distaste...A bloody affair, not one for a gentleman. She said without a change of tone: 'You realise you're committing suicide.'

'You mean that if I succeed they'll kill me?'

'That's the rule amongst the Brethren, isn't it? An eye for an eye. It's more than half of their power to terrorise.'

'That's perfectly true but I can't say I care much.' It was spoken without a hint of bravado. 'You see, I'm the last male de Var.'

For once their rapport was not immediate. 'But that makes it worse. Have you never fallen in love?'

'Once or twice.'

'And I know you've had mistresses.'

'Yes, of course.'

'Then why haven't you married and done your duty?'

'Because I don't see it that way.' He kissed her gently and held her shoulders. 'Enrica, you're my favourite woman but you're also a de Var as I am. We can't go on like this and we shan't. I don't want to see the long decline into an alien world with alien values. We're dinosaurs, we're walking dead.'

Mario rose at two in the morning, taking his motorcyle from the shed where he kept it. The old Rolls would have been too big to hide and its absence would have been noticed anyway. He drove to the hills and the airstrip, leaving the motorcycle close to the crumbling control tower.

He began to walk. There was no moon but some starlight and in any case he knew this country well. The land had been the de Vars' for centuries, which made more heinous the crime he had come to prevent.

Inside the control tower he risked a torch. He took the launcher from the cache and loaded it. Then he lay down and waited for the dawn.

By the first of its light he saw the tanker. It must have needed very skilful driving to get it onto the airstrip but there it was. Beside it was a black saloon. Four men had got out and were standing, looking west.

Mario heard the aircraft before he saw it for it was circling the airstrip cautiously, then it came into sight as it began its approach. It was a twin-engined turboprop and could carry a considerable load. The pilot brought it down professionally, then turned and taxied alongside the tanker.

Mario hadn't thought of that: it gave him a bigger and more vulnerable target. He held his breath as Charles Russell had taught him; he sighted carefully and fired at the tanker.

There was the crack of HE, then an increasing ball of fire. The aircraft, the tanker, the four men and the aircraft's crew—all were within that private hell. Mario couldn't see inside it but he could feel the heat. For a moment he feared for himself but not for long. The ground sloped away from the ruined control tower and the flaming fuel was running downhill. As the fireball spread its height diminished and Mario could see three metal skeletons, flames still licking at their mortal wounds. The bodies were a few yards away. They had tried to run.

He began to work fast for he hadn't much time. Soon this deserted, once innocent airstrip would be alive with police and the merely curious. He had been wearing gloves but he wiped the launcher. He put it back in the cache but he didn't clean it. He didn't think it would be used again. The whole area would be thoroughly searched. The cache would be found but that didn't matter.

It was now full daylight and he had to get home. Already he could hear approaching cars. Mario slipped into the scrub behind him, running to where he had left his motorcycle. He drove back to Castel del Var by a roundabout route. On the way he passed a roadside shrine and he stopped and said a prayer for the men he had killed. He didn't pray for himself since he hadn't a need to. The Almighty was a gentleman and he'd understand perfectly.

He then remounted and started to sing. It

135

was one of King David's triumphant psalms and he sang it to a Gregorian chant he'd learnt at school.

For the next few days he walked armed and warily for he knew that Frank Loretto could act fast. But when the blow which he had expected came it fell in a way he had not foreseen.

It was one of the Baron's remaining pleasures to sit on the bench at the top of his noble stairs and watch the scene below on market days. Today it was even more vivid than usual for it was a saint's day too and the crowd was in its festival clothes.

The jeep with three men drove in through the archway. The action wasn't popular with the crowd which resented wheeled traffic: it spoilt the fun. There were jeeps and catcalls, but finally the crowd made way for the jeep to turn. It drove back towards the archway, exchanging pleasantries with the now mollified crowd, and as it came to the foot of the stairs it stopped.

One man stood up with a heavy machine pistol and the burst made a pulp of the Baron's head.

In the second of shocked silence which followed the jeep drove away.

The funeral was very grand indeed. Four black horses drew the flower-covered hearse, fully caparisoned, their black plumes nodding. Behind it walked the Baron's four children, the women in black again and heavily veiled. Mario in a morning coat. Behind them came a platoon of relations, then a company of servants and tenants. Behind that was an army of locals. The cortège stretched across the square, under the archway and into the little town. The archbishop took the service himself and the funeral feast was long and elaborate.

When it was all over at last Mario de Var began to relax. He had been fretting at the enforced inaction but it would have been unthinkable not to honour his father. He said goodbye to the last of the interminable file of guests and saw his two elder sisters into their cars. Enrica had remained to the last. She was wearing her habit as was proper and seemly and her hands were folded meekly in front of her. But her expression was very far from meek. She looked at her brother, said softly: 'Well?'

'I shall do what I must.'

'Then God go with you.'

He kissed her and went upstairs to change. He had already packed and ordered a taxi. He had a fever which he knew would get worse but

137

he wouldn't stay longer in Castel del Var. He had briefed his attorney and said goodbye to the servants. When the taxi came he directed it to the airport. He had sent a large draft to an English bank and he had booked on the evening flight to London.

9

When Mario had told his story that morning he had been weak from the fever still but his head had been clear. Charles Russell listened in total silence.

He supposed he should feel at least some embarrassment but in fact he felt no regret at all. A moralist might point out sternly that it was he who had given Mario arms and that everything else had flowed from that. But in Charles Russell's view that was sloppy thinking. When Mario had fired his grenade it was certain that he had known the consequences, which were simply that his own life was forfeit; he couldn't have guessed that they would murder his father. That had been a classic soft target but a derogation from the accepted code which had demanded Mario's early death. Killing a frail old man, his father, was no sort of discharge to an honourable Brother. I distinguish, Russell thought, and checked himself...How many angels can dance on the point of a pin? If he started on the schoolmen's logic Mario, who'd been to a Catholic school, would chop him into very small pieces. Besides, there was no need to do so. What was facing him now was beyond all argument, the imperative of the ancestral blood feud, a man's private sense of his personal honour.

It would have been humbug to have pretended otherwise for Russell's own great-grandfather had fought a duel. And it hadn't been about a killing nor even about some disputed woman: it had been about a couple of farms which Russell's forebear considered had been bequeathed under duress. For that he had been prepared to kill or to die.

Russell knew he was in no position to moralise even if that had suited his temperament. He thought of Frank Loretto with horror, a man who had corrupted thousands. Perhaps that was irrelevant morally but it did make a difference to a pragmatist's thinking. Mario must have come here for help, at the very least for experienced counsel, and Russell had decided to give it. Certainly give it to a godson he liked. But first there was something he was entitled to be sure about.

He asked: 'Are you sure it was Loretto who gave the order to kill?'

'No Sicilian Brother would kill my father.'

'True. But not conclusive.'

'Then the men in that jeep were heard speaking Italian. They spoke it with an American accent. Four men caught the evening flight to New York. A jeep was found abandoned at the airport.'

'Much better.'

'And to my mind what sews it up beyond doubt is that there were flowers in Loretto's name at the funeral. Great masses of white lilies and roses. Nobody but an American gangster would do that. It's purest Twenties in Chicago or Cicero. No Sicilian Brother would conceive such an insult.'

'What did you do with them?'

'I had them burnt publicly.'

Charles Russell thought this a little extravagant. Some hospital would have taken them gladly. But then he wasn't a Sicilian nobleman.

'Very well, so it was Frank Loretto. He couldn't have thought your father destroyed that aeroplane. But he killed him instead of you. Quite outside the rules, a decadence. But why are you here?'

'I need your help.'

'I gathered that.'

'I need to know where Loretto is. I found out quite easily that he'd come to England and it's none of my business what mischief he came for. But I also know that he's not here now. He has vanished.'

'Not quite,' Russell said.

'You know where he is?'

'But I cannot tell you.'

'In that case I have been intruding rudely.'

Mario started to rise but Russell waved him down again; he said with a faint edge of asperity: 'You should listen more carefully. I said ''I cannot tell you''. Present tense. I didn't say I never would. But I need another's permission to do so and yours to tell him what you've told me. For I've an interest in Loretto, too. Not a personal one like yours but political. Very political—at this moment critical. It's just possible we could serve each other's ends.'

'And who do you want to tell?'

'A man called Lord George. Of course he has a surname too but nobody in his world uses it. He's my successor in the Security Executive.'

'Is he secure?'

'By definition. I'll make an appointment to see him tomorrow. You just stay here and rest yourself quietly. Malaria takes more out of you than you know. We'll start on Friday—that is

141

if I'm successful with Lord George.'

'*We'll* start?'

'I'm coming too.'

Charles Russell was received as became him, which was as an elder and experienced statesman, but with a good deal less disbelief than he had feared. He would have tolerated the traditional cliché that one needed a very long spoon to sup with the devil; he would have accepted, too, a tactful reminder that he wasn't as young as once he had been. Instead Lord George had listened carefully, saying at the end: 'One chance in a hundred but well worth taking.'

It wasn't at all the expected comment and Russell looked both surprised and relieved. Lord George noticed both and began to explain.

So when he'd spent that night on the telephone to America he'd learnt more than who controlled the *Compagnie Générale;* he'd learnt much about how the Brethren worked. They weren't like an ordinary firm or society where if the head man died someone else was elected. They much more closely resembled the unregenerate Tory party where, if the leader fell, somebody must 'emerge'; and where in the process there would be bitter political in-fighting before he or she did. It was exactly the same with the new boss of the Brethren except that the in-fighting would be real and bloody. It wouldn't be political heads in the basket but real ones.

All this took a considerable time and time was what the Executive needed. Moreover the new boss might not approve Loretto's plan. His death would have raised the strongest suspicion that the plan had been blown and was therefore no longer viable. Yes, Loretto's death would be manna from heaven. But it sounded a very long shot indeed. How formidable was this Mario de Var?

'I told you what he did at that airstrip.'

'Competent and also brave. But putting your name on the list for reprisals is not the same thing as killing Loretto. Has this man of yours any sort of training?'

'None. The thing he's really good at is swimming.'

'Hardly likely to be useful here. And Loretto never moves without a guard. Also that Aldo who's much more than a secretary. If you're going too, and I cannot stop you, you ought to know more about him.'

'Please.'

Then John Aldo was a qualified lawyer though he seldom gave Loretto legal advice.

He was in practice the Chief of Staff, who would be making the arrangements in Belgium where there was already an organisation for drugs. Frank Loretto himself would stay in the background, a half-mythical figure but universally feared. And Aldo was as different from Loretto as the wide spectrum of the States could provide. Loretto had fought himself up from the gutter, basically an old-fashioned gangster, except that he dealt in more deadly merchandise. But the Aldos had been long in the land and John Aldo had been schooled in New England. He had the brains and the contacts and Loretto needed them but he resented his dependence bitterly. He was persistently rude to his Chief of Staff, an ill-bred man's method of trying to get back at him.

'All this,' Lord George explained, 'came to me from America. Where I have the excellent sources you once had yourself. And something else of perhaps greater interest. It is whispered —oh, very softly whispered—that John Aldo would not be entirely displeased to find himself the next boss of the Brethren. For a man of his background that would be unprecedented but we know that the American Brethren have greatly changed. It isn't inconceivable. Not quite.'

'So there's a possible chink in Loretto's armour?'

'In theory. Very much in theory.'

Lord George's manner changed as he moved back to facts. He had given all the information he owned but there were one or two loose ends and he tied them. 'Where are you going to stay?'

'The Royal George.'

'That's where most of the English go. It's comfortable. You'll find Molly Grant is there already.'

'With her block?'

'I didn't give her one. I considered it but decided against it. You know how she takes her exercise and so do I. If it came to a question of roughing her up I'd be sorry for the man who tried it, and if it came to a man on a roof-top with sniper's sights no block in the world can protect from that. But I don't see why they should try to kill her. They're more likely to go for her contact, van Eyck.'

'Logical,' Russell said. 'And communications?'

'None unless there's a genuine crisis. We have a stringer in Ostend, an ex-operator. He's too old for anything active or dangerous' (as you should be. Lord George thought, but certainly aren't) 'but he does have a means to

145

transmit what's important. And there's a first-class man who's trying to find *Belinda*. He reaches me through the stringer. So far a blank.'

'Will you tell me how I can contact the stringer?'

'No. I'm not sending you to Ostend—you're not my man. The time might very easily come when I'd be pleased to swear I'd had nothing to do with you.'

'Fair enough,' Russell said. He'd have done the same.

He started to rise but Lord George stopped him. 'What sort of man is this Mario de Var, this so-convenient killer you found on your doorstep?'

'I told you what he did at that airstrip.'

'I meant the man himself.'

'Early forties.'

'Good-looking?'

'Very, in a Latin way.'

'And Molly Grant will be staying in the same hotel.'

Russell didn't comment: none was required. Doctor Molly Grant was an eminent scientist but a woman with notably catholic tastes. Lord George went on quietly: 'It might be an advantage.'

'It might.'

'Or it might be just another disaster.'

'*Another* disaster? You're already expecting one?'

'Of course I am. This whole affair is totally crazy. It defies every rule in the book of words.'

'In my own time—'

'Yes, I know. Good luck.'

When Russell had gone Lord George sighed softly. There were several strands in this particular ravel and each of them had a different colour. Taking Molly Grant first, she might be lucky. If Professor van Eyck should admit to her that the company on whose Board he sat was going to move active nuclear waste from its sites to the hold of a secret ship then it would be possible to convey a warning. The Belgian government would deny all knowledge but it might freeze the dangerous beast in its lair until somehow it could be otherwise tamed. There'd be an awkward period in diplomatic relations but nothing like the major incident if *Belinda* were found to be loaded and ready to sail.

In which case the man who was trying to find her was the most important strand in the tangle. Lord George had heard from him but nothing definite, and if he did would take no action himself. But he would go straight to the Prime Minister and the Prime Minister would be obliged to act. At that meeting at Number

Ten he'd been edgy, emphasising the awesome consequences of forcibly boarding a foreign ship. But if it came to the crunch Lord George didn't doubt him. If *Belinda* were found her harbour would be watched round the clock; and if she put to sea she'd be stopped.

Lord George permitted a smile at the thought ...The Royal Navy grappling a resisting vessel, ratings boarding her in protective clothing. Would they be carrying cutlasses? If somebody didn't stop them they might try. It was a scene out of a superior comic but also one of deadly seriousness.

But the Prime Minister would have to stage it in some form. The alternative of an East Anglian Chernobyl was something which he could never accept.

So that was how it looked like ending. It was true that two new actors had stepped on stage, Charles Russell and his mad Sicilian, it was also true that Loretto's death would probably abort the disaster's birth.

But that death was a pipe dream: Lord George had no faith in it.

No faith, perhaps, but a faint stirring of hope, and that hope lay in his knowledge of Russell. On the face of it what he was doing was simple: he had a godson of whom he appeared to be fond and he was taking his duties as godfather seriously. Mario was sworn to a personal vendetta and Russell had felt it a god-father's duty to prevent him throwing his life away uselessly in some hopeless attempt on that of Loretto.

Hm. Convincing and very probably final with nine men out of ten. But not Russell. He had a streak of bloody-mindedness, a Pro-testant Anglo-Irishman's conviction, not of right and wrong, mere subjective semantics, but of a real life outrage which couldn't be tolerated. It had cost him his chair at the Security Executive for he'd been very close behind a VIP. Perhaps 'eminent' rather than merely 'important' for he hadn't been a politi-cian and certainly not an ordinary spy. It would have been impossible to pursue him in Her Majesty's courts—some men, some places must be Caesar's wife—but what he had done had been to Russell intolerable and he had pressed with all the prestige he commanded that this man should be sent on an indefinite holiday. Some medical reason could be found very easi-ly. He could visit his ancestors' country quite reasonably, the country whose interests he had been shamefully serving.

But the Prime Minister of the day had not agreed. He had coveted a very high honour, one seldom given to men of his background, and he wouldn't have the least chance of getting it if he did as Charles Russell and others were urging. He didn't dismiss Charles Russell—he didn't dare. That, in a rather different way, would have raised as much dust as what Russell was insisting on. But nor had he any need to dismiss him. His five-year term was ending shortly and the Prime Minister simply had not renewed it. Charles Russell, still plain Colonel Russell, had gone into early retirement with dignity.

Lord George thought this incident significant to the present. Charles Russell could stick his heels in like a mule...Frank Loretto? Traffic in drugs? He'd have the ordinary decent man's horror of both but they might not blow the firm fuse which controlled him. But if Loretto stepped outside Russell's pale, did something which really outraged his ethos, then there'd be two vendettists in Belgium, not one.

10

The aircraft to Ostend had been cramped, crowded, insanitary and late, and Russell and Mario de Var were both in bad tempers when they arrived at the Royal George hotel. They went out to eat, returning to an early bed, and at breakfast next morning saw Molly Grant. She was eating at another table and gave Russell a glance of recognition but made no move to join them till they stood. When they did so she brought her tray to their table.

Charles Russell introduced de Var. 'This is Mario de Var, my godson. He's here to murder Frank Loretto.' It was a calculated throwaway but Molly took it without a visible blink. 'And the lady is Doctor Molly Grant. She's an eminent nuclear physicist who specialises in micro-radio-activity. But her interest here is in something more dangerous.' When Molly looked surprised he added: 'Mario has been told the whole story and Lord George knows he's here with me.'

'Then welcome to the club,' she said. 'So far it hasn't been wildly successful.'

She was disposing of a plateful of croissants which she ate with butter and cherry jam. Mario was discreetly staring for the overload of carbohydrates didn't go with a finely disciplined figure, but then he couldn't possibly know that she took her regular exercise by playing it rough in a Martial Arts school. She was looking at Mario in a way Russell recognised, not the look which the blue rinses gave to him, the 'I wonder' look which he briskly resented, but something much more open and earthy. Mario was a handsome man in a not overly Mediterranean way, unmistakably male with a hint of arrogance, enough to challenge a sophisticated woman. An attraction would be in no way surprising, indeed Lord George had come close to foretelling it.

Molly had finished her generous breakfast. 'I'm here on Number Ten's account—in both senses of that elastic word—so I've allowed myself a sitting-room too. I think we'd better go up and talk.'

It was a pleasant little unpompous room and looked out across a busy square. There was a refrigerator but it was early for drinks, and a glass contraption for making coffee. Molly offered it but they shook their heads. There was also an outsize television set which she dismissed with a wave of the hand with a glove on it. 'That set receives five countries easily and all the programmes are equally silly.' She looked at Russell in silent enquiry and when he didn't answer asked: 'You said your godson knew our side of the story. Hadn't you better tell me his?'

'I did. He's here to murder Frank Loretto.'

'You didn't tell me why.'

Russell looked at Mario who nodded back. 'You tell her, please,' he said.

Charles Russell did so. He had a gift of matter-of-fact exegesis and he made the story sound almost banal. Throughout it Molly watched Mario closely, her expression changing from open astonishment to something which it was harder to read. At the end she asked a single question.

'And you have to do the killing yourself. Just having it done would not be enough?'

'It would not.'

Doctor Molly Grant, a Dame if she'd wished to be, eminent in nuclear science and preeminent in her own strange branch of it, had always worn her honours lightly and for a moment they'd been quite forgotten in an emotion which had made her shiver. When that was past she said collectedly: 'On my side I haven't been very successful. I've met Professor van Eyck for a chat and he has confirmed what we

153

already suspected. This country is bursting with nuclear waste and it embarrasses the government greatly. To get rid of it responsibly could cost huge sums of money, and they daren't put up taxes or cut social services. So there's every temptation to take a short cut or at least to turn a blind eye to its taking. But as a member of the CG's Board Julius van Eyck hasn't leaked. Though I'm convinced he knows and is frightened stiff. Perhaps given a little more time which we haven't got...'

'You've reported this?' Russell asked.

'Through the embassy. The Prime Minister gave them orders to transmit for me. They didn't like it a bit and they showed it.'

'They would,' Russell said. 'They'd think it beneath their professional dignity, though the last Prime Minister did a lot to cut them down to size. What happened?'

'I saw a Secretary-man first. He flatly refused. So I pulled rank a bit and reached someone more senior. He protested but in the end he sent.'

'Do you think you were followed? Either there or with van Eyck?'

'I don't know.'

'Of course she was followed.' It was Mario de Var, and when they looked surprised he explained. 'It would be sensible, wouldn't it?

154

They may suspect that van Eyck is a potential bad risk and if so he'll be under surveillance already. Since you've been meeting him you'll have been noticed too. It would be perfectly simple to find out who you were. And very suspicious indeed that would look to them.'

Charles Russell had been doing some thinking. 'This "they" of yours,' he said. 'Tell us more. You came here to kill Frank Loretto himself, so presumably you've done some research.'

Mario said that he hadn't needed to: Frank Loretto's form was generally known. He had a standing organisation in Belgium but he wouldn't have gone near it himself. It was his habit, indeed his private conceit, to stay in the shadows, a figure of mystery, building up his mystique and above all fear of him. Any necessary contacts would be made by John Aldo who in fact was Loretto's effective brains. And, of course, there'd be a third man, a guard. Ostensibly two rich men's manservant.

And what would be these rich men's cover?

Simple. They'd be well-to-do businessmen on the spree. They would be staying at the Grand in a suite, probably having most meals sent up to them. But no women with them, not even the smell of one. That sort of flash had gone out with bootleg hooch. Your modern

Brother was almost painfully uxorious.

So how did these rich Transatlantics amuse themselves?

They would do all the things which Ostend offered. They weren't the type to crawl round the bars—their drinking, if any, would be modest and private—but they'd do the standard trips to the Flemish towns. They were prosperous now on American money but as chocolate-box picturesque as ever. And then they would probably swim, though not in the sea. The shelving beach was superb for children but at low tide you had to walk a mile before an adult could find enough water to swim in. But there was one of the best sea pools in the world.

And finally they would certainly gamble. The Casino was not in Loretto's class but though he didn't travel with women he liked to flash his money in public and in any case was a devoted gambler. Yes, they'd find him at the Casino for certain.

'So we're going out to meet the enemy.' It was Molly Grant and the 'we' was deliberate. But at the same time she spoke with a certain doubt. She understood the itch for immediate action but wondered if that were the best course open. 'If we identify them they'll identify us and the only advantage Mario has is that they'll

156

hardly have discovered that he's here.' She turned to Russell. 'What do you think?'

He took his time in answering and his answer left the choice to them. 'It's a balance of disadvantages.' He looked at Mario. 'If they see you with Doctor Grant you're blown. They won't necessarily guess what you've really come for but Doctor Grant is already suspect of trying to break down Professor van Eyck so at the lowest you'll be suspect of that too. On the other hand you'll get nowhere whatever by holing up in this hotel indefinitely. To put it in the most brutal terms you have a very poor chance of killing Loretto. If you stay hidden in the Royal George you have none. Take your pick.'

'In practice there isn't a choice.'

'Just so.'

'Then you've been here before, sir, and know the form. What time does the Casino open?'

'At noon on the dot. And I'm coming too.'

Mario objected. 'You may be recognised.'

'It might just conceivably pay if I were. A father-figure sometimes has uses.'

The Casino was a long way from the Principality's grandeurs, and even longer from the extravagances of Las Vegas. But it was a

157

pleasant little establishment, properly solemn, furnished in the repro Louis Quinze beloved of the Belgian *haute bourgeoisie*. At opening time it wasn't yet crowded. There was the usual scatter of local expatriates, sitting at the bottom of the table, playing their incomprehensible systems, trying to make an extra bottle of gin. On the far side sat three men in sober clothes. The guard looked like an athletic valet. Aldo wore an expensive lightweight suit and Loretto a double-breasted blazer. This Charles Russell considered a mistake. Even sitting he looked smaller than average and a double-breaster did nothing to help him.

Russell, Molly and Mario stood and watched; they watched for some time before the other three noticed them and Aldo was the first to do so. He stared at Mario in blank astonishment, then he touched Loretto's arm and said something into the ear which was nearest him. Frank Loretto looked up in turn and glowered. At no time were his features distinguished but in anger they were almost simian. Presently he shrugged and went back to his chips. John Aldo gave Molly a polite little bow.

Loretto had been playing *en plein*— the maximum. By the standards of other and bigger casinos that maximum could be considered modest but it was a good deal of money to most

158

of those present. Frank Loretto was attracting attention and it was evident that he wasn't averse to it. He kept the maximum on Seventeen, expressionless when he steadily lost his stake. He was trying to create an impression and he was: he was a rich man taking his pleasure indifferently. The others at the table watched enviously.

He had four more losses and then the number came up. The croupier pushed the winnings across with his rake. They were in a single enormous plaque rarely seen. Loretto casually picked it up and put it back on Seventeen.

The croupier began to explain politely... But Monsieur must understand that the maximum...

He knew all about the maximum, thank you. But in every self-respecting casino there was a convention that if a man won *en plein* he could leave his winnings on the number they'd stuck on.

Not in this one.

Then send for the manager.

The croupier had already done so for there was a button below the table, which he'd pressed. He'd seen plenty of trouble from loutish tourists but this was a variation of insolence which he hadn't been exposed to before.

The manager appeared at once. He wore a morning coat and a flower in his buttonhole and he was very self-possessed indeed. He had every reason to be self-possessed. Casinos in Belgium were state monopolies and he himself a civil servant. He had only to press another button and plain clothes police would appear very quickly. If a troublemaker went quietly well and good but if he threw his weight about he was liable to get hurt quite badly. The manager had pressed his button too.

He bowed to Frank Loretto urbanely. He understood there was some little difficulty.

There bloody was. Frank Loretto had made his demand in fair faith for he owned a casino where that convention did operate. (And very profitable it had proved to the house.) But he knew that it wasn't by any means general and he hadn't intended to press it too seriously. But this elderly Belgian's composure angered him. He began to shout and wave his hands. Standing you could see his built-up shoes. So he'd been cheated by a two-bit provincial box.

A curious crowd had begun to form and the manager knew that crowds could be fickle but his manner of cool aplomb didn't waver. Monsieur would gain nothing whatever by using such intemperate language.

Aldo and the guard had risen too, standing

160

one each side of Loretto. The guard looked at the elderly Belgian. 'Shall I take him?' he enquired.

'Certainly not.' It had been Aldo and he had spoken decisively. He put a hand on Frank Loretto's shoulder. 'Cool it,' he said. Unmistakably it was an order. He was Loretto's servant but in a crisis his master. Loretto knew it and resented it bitterly.

'I'll be—'

'Probably not that but you will be in prison. And that isn't going to help us at all.'

Four men had come through the Casino's doors and were standing in a compact little knot; they were looking at the manager, waiting for the signal to act. Aldo touched Loretto again and nodded at the four men by the door. 'You haven't a hope in hell,' he said.

The dangerous tension had begun to relax, the curious to drift away. Most were relieved but a few disappointed. In the silence John Aldo had been staring at Russell. The look had held more than a single meaning but Russell had read them both correctly. Charles Russell looked the sort of man who would find any public scene distasteful and this American was signalling strongly that he found it out of order himself. He was apologising.

And the second message was rather less

obvious since it was one of a despairing lone-
liness. John Aldo worked for a professional
criminal but what he wanted at this moment
in time was a chat with another civilised man.
He glanced at the bar and half-raised his eyebrows.

Charles Russell nodded unhesitatingly.

He turned to Mario de Var beside him. 'I
suggest you take Molly to lunch. To my taste
the best place by far is the Chopin.'

'It is,' she said. 'I've been there already.
Before you arrived.'

'Have you indeed? Then don't discuss business.'

They said together: 'I wasn't going to.'

'The *sole flamande* is superb.'

'I know.'

Russell watched them go out arm-in-arm. So
Lord George had been right as he often was.
It remained to be seen if good would come of
it.

He was conscious that the guard and Loretto
were standing apart in apparent uncertainty,
watching the knot of men which was still by
the door. He wanted to talk to the man at
the bar and he didn't want unwelcome intru-
sions. He walked over to them and nodded
politely.

'Gentlemen, the party is over. You can go.

162

No one has any interest in stopping you.'

'And who in hell are you?'

'You could call me a friend of the new Baron de Var.' Russell nodded again and joined Aldo at the bar.

Loretto and the guard hesitated but finally moved. None of the men at the door tried to stop them. One of them took a photograph and that was all. Outside they walked twenty paces, then halted. Loretto said furiously:

'Those three at the table. You know who they were?'

'The woman we've been shadowing since she contacted that Professor van Eyck. One of the other men was Mario de Var.'

'What's *he* doing here with the woman? And the other man?'

'Stranger to me.'

Frank Loretto scowled for he didn't approve. Here was a man whom none of them knew, from the company he was keeping at least a potential enemy, and the first thing that egg-head Aldo does is to sit on a stool and drink with him socially. It was the sort of too-clever thing he *would* do.

But that would have to be dealt with later. For the moment there were de Var and the woman. 'You heard that talk about lunch at the Chopin?'

'Sure.'

'And that she'd been there before?'

'She has. So Mr Aldo has had it covered.'

It was always 'Mr Aldo' between them. That was part of the established protocol.

'Then listen very carefully. I don't want any more bright boy screw-ups. How did Aldo fix it?'

'A waiter.'

The guard noticed there had been no 'Mister'. He wasn't bright but he had a peasant's sharp instincts. This was a derogation of protocol. These weren't the words which he used to himself but John Aldo was clearly fading in favour and with a man like Loretto that wasn't healthy.

'Then this waiter reports to you and you to me. Bring it to me on a plate and quick.'

'Okay.'

Charles Russell slipped onto the stool beside Aldo. 'Good morning,' he said. 'My name is Charles Russell.'

If Aldo was astonished he hid it. 'I'm very greatly honoured, sir.' He had slid off his stool for a small formal bow, which gave Russell a better chance to observe him. He had already noticed the expensive two-piece suit, the exactly right amount of cuff, the air of almost presidential well grooming. But now he noticed something else. Unlike Mr President's the clothes were old-fashioned. The coat had a single slit, not two, and the closely-cut trousers had turn-ups. Turn-ups! They were hopelessly unfashionable but very, very Ivy League.

John Aldo had got back onto his stool. 'May I offer you a drink, sir?'

'That's kind. What are you drinking yourself?'

'Whisky and soda.'

Not scotch on the rocks. Good marks again. Russell seldom drank whisky before his luncheon but said: 'May I have the same?'

'Of course.'

The barman poured the drink and Russell said: 'Your good health.'

'Your very good health, sir.'

More good marks.

'You must forgive me that I didn't recognise you.' John Aldo laughed. 'You have the reputation of having been photographed rarely. My name is John Aldo and I work for Frank Loretto. The other man with us is his guard, block or hoodlum. I find him very boring company.'

Charles Russell was enjoying himself: these deliberate formalities pleased him. 'And Frank Loretto?' he asked.

'I said that I worked for him.'

Russell ordered more drinks and Aldo went on. 'But I have the advantage of you and that is discourteous. You see, I know who your two companions are already. One is Doctor Molly Grant, a nuclear scientist of world standing and a specialist in micro-radiation. The other is called Mario de Var.'

'Whose father was recently murdered in public.'

'You must believe me that I was greatly against it but you cannot teach old dogs new tricks.' Aldo took a pull at his drink and with it he became almost reflective. 'Violence I will accept since I must—even killings. Terror is part of my master's armoury and often it is regrettably necessary. But killings for pure revenge I deplore. I am not an Israeli.'

'So I observe. But aren't you being a little indiscreet?'

'I don't think so. We're both of us in the same hard trade.'

'How do you work that out?'

'Very easily. Frank Loretto is a world-class criminal and sometimes his crimes spill over into politics. Your business was to confound such offences.'

'I like "confound".'

'I think it is accurate. And now may we be

a little less formal?'

'Just as you wish.'

Aldo's manner altered at once but though the almost anglicised English didn't change the idiom did. 'Watch it, Colonel,' he said. 'Please watch it.'

'Oh, I do.'

'I haven't insulted you by telling you we're here on holiday, though we try to give that impression by doing the holiday things. But we are not. And you are here with Mario de Var.'

'I'm his godfather. His honorary godfather.'

'I know that. And how it came about.'

'You know a great deal.'

'It's what I'm paid for. You could call me the top Brothers' eyes and ears. And, of course, I can talk to people they cannot.'

'Such as myself?'

'The perfect example. And on the side I try to civilise when I can. Not very successfully. Loretto and the two or three like him came up from the gutter the gutter way. And they're the most rigid of traditionalists. Use the word "difficulty" and they'll use the word "kill". That's why I ask you to watch it carefully. I'm a Chief of Staff. I don't command.'

'I'll watch it, all right.'

'Then a drink on that?'

'Thank you, no. I've had my ration.'

'So have I. I like alcohol but I detest getting fuddled.' John Aldo slid off his stool again and his formal manner returned as he did so. 'Would you do me the honour of lunching one day?'

'With very great pleasure.' It had been spoken unhesitatingly.

'Normally we eat in our hotel. But I don't imagine you'd fancy the company.'

'No.'

'But I heard you recommend the Chopin.'

'Then you also heard me tell my friends not to talk business.'

'You were perfectly right. We've been watching Doctor Molly Grant ever since she made contact with Professor van Eyck, and now that de Var has appeared on the scene naturally he will be tailed even closer. What is said at the Chopin today will reach me. On the other hand when it's just you and me I can guarantee a total privacy.'

'You earn your money.'

'I try to give value. Then shall we say Wednesday at half-past twelve?'

'I'll look forward to it very much.'

'So shall I. So don't disappoint me—don't do anything foolish. I repeat if I may: I am not the boss.'

11

By now Molly Grant was almost an established customer and the Chopin's *patron* received
her with proper deference. He led her, Mario
a step behind, to the table which she had had
the last time but he didn't bother to show
the menu. He remembered what she had had
before and was paying her the compliment of
assuming she'd order the same again. But he
showed the wine list to Mario de Var. 'The
white Macon goes very well with Madame's
sole.'

They wasted no time on exchanging backgrounds for the important decision had been
taken without words. Both of them knew it and
neither wished to pry. Mario watched Molly
eat with frank gusto. Presently he said: 'May
I risk an impertinence?'

'If it isn't a real one.'

'Then how do you keep that magnificent
figure?'

'I take exercise.' She told him how.

'Unarmed combat,' he said. 'A good idea.
Much better than that silly boxing. Queensberry

169

rules and all that nonsense. It's useless against a serious attack.'

'You boxed at your English school?'

'I wasn't any good at games so I was *made* to box. I wasn't any use at that either. I didn't even have my house colours, but I did get my school colours. Just like that.'

Molly Grant smelt a story. English public schools were eccentric and the Catholic ones more peculiar than most. 'Tell,' she said.

'So we used to have matches against other schools, and in those days *the* boxing school was St Paul's. Just as Lancing had been *the* sports school. Running, skipping, hopping and jumping—all that. These matches were eight or ten contests a side at various weights. One point for an appearance, two for a draw and three for a win on points. Nobody was ever knocked out—they stopped a fight if a boy was in trouble. Now at some weight or other, rather an odd one, our proper man had gone down with measles. Since I was that weight and technically a boxer I was asked to take his place. One point. It wasn't the sort of school where you could say No.'

'They put you up as a sacrifice but you won?'

'I won on a flagrant foul.'

'Weren't you disqualified?'

'Nearly but not quite.' He looked at her in

170

certain doubt but she was genuinely interested, even amused. He suspected that her sense of humour was very nearly as black as his own. 'So when I got into the ring at the venue— wearing a vest, of course: that was *de rigueur* I found that the boy I was boxing was coloured. I didn't object to that, I couldn't, but I did object to the way he fought. He was in a totally different class from me and could hit me more or less as he liked. I knew that was going to happen and took it but he was doing it so as to make me look a fool. At the end of the round I had black eyes and a bleeding nose and I could see they were in two minds about letting it go on. But they did.'

'What happened then?'

'The coloured boy started to laugh at me openly. I lost my temper.'

Molly Grant approved but silently. Men who couldn't lose their tempers were known to be uninteresting partners. She said: 'Go on.'

'So I forgot about boxing and started to brawl. I pushed him up against the ropes and started hitting him wherever I could. In public school boxing there's no referee in the ring so there was nobody to break us up physically. The coloured boy started to yell blue murder, or he did till I caught him with the heel of my hand. He fell down cold.'

'And then?'

'There was a stricken sort of silence. We were on the wrong side of the judges so they didn't see the actual foul punch but plenty of other people did. The officials started to buzz like blowflies. Most had seen that I'd been fighting rough but they'd disapproved even more of the coloured boy's yelling. That simply wasn't done in school boxing.'

'So you got away with it?'

'Just. And there was a convention that if you won against St Paul's you got your school colours. I was given them with due pomp and ceremony but I was never asked to box again.'

'Happy ending,' she said.

'In a rum sort of way.'

'I like things rum.'

'I'm delighted to hear it.'

She took a long pull at her glass which finished it and Mario ordered another bottle. When her glass was full again she went on. 'And talking of things being rum, that school of yours—'

'It was worse than rum; it was squalid and evil. Spying was common, indeed encouraged. You see, the school was run by monks.'

'Which Order?'

'I can't tell you that. It would tell you which school.'

She was pleased again but discreetly hid it.

172

This sort of loyalty might be embarrassingly old-fashioned but any loyalty was still a virtue. 'Then were you unhappy at school?' she asked.

'I was at first but I soon learned to be cunning.'

'Weren't you that anyway?' She had smiled as she said it.

'The de Vars have been around for some time: naturally we're not actively stupid. What I learnt was a specialised English cunning. How to get enough sleep, as a simple example. If I can get it I like a solid ten hours.'

Many virile men did, she thought, and said: 'So do I.'

'And the good fathers thought ten hours sybaritic. It gave pleasure and was therefore suspect. Sneaking up to the dormitory by day was a beating offence, and if another boy went with you you were automatically expelled, even if he were the ugliest in the school.'

'It sounds pretty grim.'

'I would call it dour.'

'So what did you do?'

'I learnt to catnap in chapel without being spotted. Twice a day. In passing, that's one reason I'm fond of Charles Russell. When he took me away on exeats he never mentioned theatres or cinemas; he just gave me enormous meals and let me sleep.'

173

'So you'll take a siesta this afternoon?'

'After all this food and drink I'll have to.'

'An excellent idea,' she said. 'I'll join you.'

It was ambiguous and intended to be so, a probe. She could see that he understood her but if he followed up too closely he'd disappoint. He didn't disappoint but said coolly:

'And in the evening we might go to the swimming pool.'

'If you're not otherwise engaged.'

'How should I be?'

'I thought you came here to kill Frank Loretto.' There was irony in the voice but no malice.

'And now that may have to wait a while.'

She looked at him sharply and they both of them laughed. He paid the bill and they left arm-in-arm again.

And the waiter, who'd been more attentive than ever, slipped out at the back and ran fast to a telephone. The number he rang had been altered an hour ago but he was very well paid and hadn't questioned the change.

Frank Loretto was saying to the guard, block or hoodlum: 'So de Var and the woman are going swimming this evening.'

'That's what I've just got from the waiter.' He looked at Frank Loretto expectantly. 'You want them eliminated?' It was a word he'd acquired from watching telly. Now he worked it to death and annoyed Frank Loretto.

'That would be premature,' Loretto said. It was a word he had acquired from John Aldo.

'Then roughed-up a bit?'

'Not yet.' Loretto wished Aldo were present to hear him. Aldo thought him just another gangster; he'd show him he could be as smart as he was. 'Doctor Grant has been seeing van Eyck—right?'

'Right.'

'And she's living in a hotel.'

'What of it?'

'Where she won't have an office.'

'I just don't get it.'

'You should. She's been seeing van Eyck and we don't know what he's told her. If he's talked we may have to work faster than I like. We have to have that and you're going to get it.'

'But I thought you said not to rough her up.'

Loretto sighed with an exaggerated patience. If Aldo thought Loretto a thug then he in turn thought this thug a numbskull. 'She may be a high-up scientist but she's also a woman.'

'Sure she is.'

'And she hasn't got an office.'

'You said so.'

175

'Then anything she's got will be in her bag. Go out and get it and bring it to me.'

'Tonight?'

'When else?'

When the guard had gone Frank Loretto lit a slightly showy cigar; he thought again of his servant John Aldo. It couldn't go on like this—not for long. He was inventive, meticulous of detail, and he could organise; he could also talk to people Frank Loretto could not. The perfect fixer but for a single thing. He was getting too big for his handmade shoes. He'd have to go.

There were two ways to the indoor swimming pool from the Royal George, one by the road upon which it stood and the other slightly longer but pleasanter, by the sea and up some stairs to the sports complex. Mario and Molly had chosen the latter.

It wasn't yet dark but the day was fading and the crowd on the bank had begun to melt, the elderlies in their canvas chairs (some of them even brought their own), the young couples with excited children. There were impromptu games of football, even one, presumably English, of cricket. The tide was a long way out but the sands superb. On their left on the promenade, between the buttresses which held

176

its wall, there was the occasional starched nanny with an expensive pram. Above the containing wall the Edwardian baroque of the Grand hotel looked down with a plushy condescension. Mario waved a hand and said:

'That's where our friends will be staying. I'm sure of it.'

'I don't want to talk of our friends too much, though the Professor is giving me lunch tomorrow.'

'Any luck so far?'

'Yes and no. He doesn't hide that he's worried sick. We both of us know the reason why and mere confirmation wouldn't help much. But a date for *Belinda's* loading would.'

'We haven't even found *Belinda* yet.'

'I don't see why with luck we shouldn't. And if we knew where she was *and* when she was loading there'd be the option of taking some positive action.'

'Do you think there's any chance the Professor will spill?'

'Even if he knows, very little. He's running scared of what's going on but he's even more scared of his Company's masters.'

'But if he did talk there'd be an immediate crisis. Do you think the Prime Minister would face up to it squarely?'

'Yes, I do. I've worked for him for some time

177

and can read him. In any case he'd *have* to take
action. Which is the worse of two shattering
evils? Having a row with the Belgian government and possibly with NATO too or evacu-
ating half East Anglia? But I don't want to
talk any more. Let's swim.'

They climbed the staircase to the pool and
changed. Molly wore a plain black one-piece.
It was severe but showed off her full, fine
figure. On the edge of the pool she said to
Mario: 'I can swim but I'm not good at it. I
never feel really at home in water.'

'When you do it doubles or trebles the
pleasure.'

'Charles Russell told me you're a very fine
swimmer.'

'I hope he also told you it's the only thing
I do reasonably well.'

Doctor Molly permitted what came quite
close to a giggle. 'If he had it would have
been totally slanderous. Anyway, will you teach
me?'

'Gladly.'

They slipped into the water and he watched. She swam half a length breast-stroke, but
keeping her head too high for efficiency, then
broke into a clumsy crawl, bending her knees
and thrashing up a wake. He already knew she
had long slim legs and it offended him to see

178

them misapplied. 'Not like that,' he said. 'You're just wasting energy.'

'But I've got to keep my legs up.'

'Quite right. But contrary to what they tell you your legs don't give you much power without flippers. Just flutter them.'

'Flutter them?'

'Yes.' He showed her. 'Now hold the rails with your arms at full stretch. Face in the water. Turn it left or right to breathe, alternately. Just keep your legs going up and down. Bend your knees as little as possible. The idea is to keep your legs out of the way while you pull yourself along with your arms.'

Presently she said: 'This is killing me.'

'Hard on the stomach muscles?'

'I feel I've been kicked in the belly by a mule.'

'That's good.'

When she'd had enough he let her go, swimming a few lengths alone. The pool was too crowded for serious exercise but when he climbed out she smiled and said: 'You swim like a fish.'

'Hardly that, I'm afraid. But I have done a whole lot more than you have. In a week you'll be as at home as I am.'

She knew that this was untrue but was flattered.

As they walked towards the dressing room he felt her nudge him and checked his stride. 'Walk on,' she said, 'and don't look round. But our friends are here.'

'Our friends from the Grand?'

'Loretto and the man who thinks for him.'

'The hood isn't there?'

'I didn't see him.'

'I expect they feel safe enough in a crowded pool.'

'But why are they here? Swimming's hardly their thing.'

'It *has* to be—it's part of their act. They're businessmen on a jaunt abroad and they have to do the expected things. We've seen them at the Casino already. This pool is one of the town's known attractions so to visit it fits in with their cover.'

They walked home along the front again. It was almost dark now, and though there were street lamps the intervals between them were wide and one or two had been vandalised by visitors.

And out of the shadows below a buttress a man appeared and ran straight at Molly. He made a grab at her bag but she coolly dropped it. He was too close for the Glasgow handshake this time but close enough for the *ucimata*, the blistering, crushing inner hip throw. He went

180

down in a heap, still conscious but breathless. Mario had produced a knife but Molly took his right wrist and bent it. He gave a cry of pain though she'd done it gently. The knife fell on the tarmac. The figures froze.

Molly bent down and recovered her bag. From it she took a torch and flashed it. The man on the ground had got part of his breath back; he was shaky still but had started to rise.

'It's that man of Loretto's and he may have a gun. Pick up that knife and run like hell.'

12

Mario was woken at three in the morning by enormous laughter from Molly beside him. He pulled himself up on an elbow. 'Share the joke.'

'There are two of them really.' She was recovering from the worst of the spasm. 'And one of them is a joke against you.'

'Then let's have the other first.'

'That bag which Loretto's man didn't get.'

'I didn't think that funny.'

'It would have been if he'd managed to get

it. It was full of notes of my meetings with van Eyck.'

'You call that amusing?'

'It chokes me cold. They weren't notes about what's going on—I told you he'd told me nothing useful—but I was under him when he was a Professor at Leyden, and when I told him I was stuck into MCRA he was interested and gave me some ideas. People like van Eyck and myself have a private language in which we communicate—symbols in esoteric equations. You take them home and stare at them for hours. Sometimes they tell you something; sometimes they don't. The thought of Mr Frank Loretto, eager and het up for hard gen, a dream of his holding a bunch of equations is my excuse for waking you up so uncivilly.'

It was the sort of dour jest which Mario relished but not the sort which made him laugh aloud. 'And the other joke?' he enquired.

'That knife of yours.'

'What about my knife?'

'Well, isn't it...?' She hesitated, finally said: 'Isn't it a little, well, corny? It's the sort of cliché you see on the box. Sicilian baddies sticking each other with knives. But you're not a Sicilian baddie on the box. You're an educated man. Anyway, who taught you to use it?'

This time Mario de Var did laugh. 'An idle question?' he asked.

'Not at all.'

'It was my father who taught me to use a knife.'

She saw that she'd scored a *bêtise* and said: 'Sorry.'

'You couldn't have known,' he said.

'You're generous.'

She could see that he wasn't entirely mollified but to say 'Let's forget the knife' would be brash. He wasn't, thank God, what was called a sensitive, a pejorative word she shunned. She could get all the sensitivity she wanted from earnest young students with social consciences. Who bored her stiff, whereas Mario excited her. But she'd been insensitive herself and regretted it. Perhaps the best line now was the casual one, to take this man's weapon entirely for granted, to ask some casual question and let him talk. She said quietly, without further apology: 'I noticed that your knife is curved.'

She saw that she had succeeded handsomely for he answered without a hint of resentment. 'And you were thinking that I'm not an Arab?'

'Something like that.'

'But the Moors were in my country for centuries and a curving knife has a real advantage.

183

Have you ever seen a knife fight?'

'Only in a film.'

'I know the one. Cary Grant is fighting a jealous Spaniard for the person of Sophia Loren, no less. They fought it out as a sort of duel, as though they'd been fighting with swords, thrust and parry. But I'm not going to fight a duel with Loretto, I'm going to kill him by any means I may. And Loretto like other men has a rib cage.' He was naked and rolled on his back to show her. 'Here. To the right of the navel and just above it. Striking upwards. The curve of the knife takes it straight to the heart.'

Doctor Molly Grant said simply: 'I see.'

'I've realised that because I speak English, people are apt to assume I am too. In fact I come from another world, almost from another century. My roots aren't here and I can't pull them up, even if I wanted to. Which I do not.' He had been speaking with a controlled sort of passion but now his voice went back to normal; he rose on an elbow again and lay beside her. 'You should get some more sleep. You're going to need it.'

'Why now particularly?'

'I was thinking of your lunch with van Eyck. You'll need to be sharp. As you said, if we knew the date of loading...'

'I told you—I think he's too frightened to spill. In any case he's old and pretty sick. There are times when he's barely with you at all.'

When John Aldo heard of the attempt to mug Molly he swore and said something in passable German.

Against stupidity the gods themselves fight in vain.

Loretto had hoped to seem subtle, sophisticated, every bit as sharp and clever as the man he employed but had always resented. But John Aldo thought the whole plan crass...So Doctor Molly Grant was interfering, talking to Professor van Eyck who might be insecure. Killing her, the standard solution, would have been untimely since it would have attracted attention, the last thing desirable with more important matters on the boil. Even Loretto had realised that. So he decides he must know whatever she does and goes for her handbag in case it's in it.

That, on the face of it, wasn't stupid: women, even eminent women, were known to keep curious things in their handbags and Molly Grant was not a trained agent. But it was also very shallow reasoning since it totally ignored the background. *One.* Assuming Molly

185

Grant had discovered anything she would have passed it on to whoever controlled her and she'd been seen to call at the British embassy. Knowledge of what she knew was by now too late.

And *Two*, John Aldo thought contemptuously. *One* was in itself an assumption. *If* van Eyck had leaked... But had he? He wasn't an executive director; he was on the Board for his notable record. It was probable that he had nothing to leak. But he was old and frail and he and Doctor Molly Grant had a background in common. She had even been his pupil once. So if he were in the secret there was a risk he would leak it. True. Though not at once—he wasn't that feeble—but risk it remained. He, Aldo, was paid to eliminate risks. He had foresight and had applied it to his problem logically. Molly Grant was the channel for anything leaked but Professor van Eyck was inescapably the source. Why go for the channel when you could block the source?

He turned his mind to his own position. It didn't look good. Loretto had gone behind his back, ordering an act of violence without even consulting his Chief of Staff. That he had never done before. It was an omen and John Aldo could read them. Loretto had been showing an increasing dislike for him but he was his brains and his eyes and his entry into other worlds. In a word indispensable.

Which no man ever was in fact.

And even that wouldn't last for ever—no, sir. Other young men were coming up, men with more acceptable backgrounds, more typical of the Brethren's ethos. Sooner or later John Aldo would be replaced.

Replaced but that would not be the end of it. He knew far too much to be allowed just to walk away. So long as Loretto was still unquestioned boss a dismissed John Aldo would be counting his hours of life.

He remembered his luncheon date with Charles Russell. Who hadn't snapped his head off when he suggested they were both in crime. It was on record that he was often unorthodox, and though a single meeting proved nothing it might be possible to reach understanding, the classic *combinazione* of his race.

The Managing Director of the *Compagnie Générale pour la Déchargement de Déchets et d'Effluents Industriels SA.* was talking to his wife at breakfast. It had been an arranged marriage, or at the least one thoroughly approved by both families. Her grandfather had founded the *Compagnie Générale* and her father had built it into the international business it now was. His daughter had been his heir since he'd had no son. A grandson had been considered imperative and the present Managing Director, then a rising executive in one of the multi-nationals, eminently eligible to get one. Like many such marriages this one had held together for thirty prosperous years, any little personal difficulty soon dissolved in the knowledge of their common interests. He still liked his wife and admired her good sense. He also trusted her and for an excellent reason; control of the company had been sold to America but she still held more than enough of the equity to make life very hard for him if she chose. She never had but he always consulted her.

This morning he finished his coffee and said: 'I'm worried about this affair of *Belinda.*'

'I never liked it,' she said.

'Nor did I, come to that. But you know who now controls our company and you very well know what that means in practice.'

'It means that you gave in to pressure.'

'And you would not?' It was enquiry, not sarcasm.

'I didn't say that. It would have depended how much I was frightened physically.'

'I was very scared and still am.'

'You've been bearing it well, I give you that. But something new has happened, yes?'

188

Prevarication would be wholly useless: she could read his mind like a piece of typescript. 'Suppose,' he said, 'but just suppose, that the English had warning of what we intend. Which is to foul their nest as it never has been.'

'Obviously they'd take preventative action. There are several things they could do and they'd have a choice. And they're not some United Nations stateling. But why should they have any warning at all?'

'Julius van Eyck,' he said. 'He's old and he's very frail. He might leak.'

'But what knowledge would he have to leak? He's not even an executive Director.'

'Conceded. But he might have seen some paper by mistake, or more likely he just smells there's something wrong. He's old and frail, but not senile. There's been a feeling about the Boardroom recently...'

'The smell of conspiracy?'

'That puts it well.'

'Then if he hasn't seen some paper he shouldn't all he'll have to leak is conjecture.'

'Suppose there was some Englishman, somebody already suspicious. Alert him there's something wrong in the company, then, even if there aren't any facts, his suspicions are going to get very much stronger. There's going to be

189

professional prying at exactly the moment we do not want it.'

'You're hiding something,' she said.

'Not hiding it. I was keeping it for the end where it matters.' He drew a long breath and let it out slowly. 'There is such an Englishman or rather a woman. Have you heard of Doctor Molly Grant?'

She shook her head.

'She's an eminent nuclear scientist, a Fellow of the Royal Society and Advisor to the British Prime Minister on any matter of science generally. And she's here in Ostend at this moment.'

'Go on.'

'She was a pupil of van Eyck at Leyden and she's been talking to him more than once.'

She thought this over for two full minutes. 'Do our friends know this?' she asked.

'It was they who warned me. They've been having her watched.'

She thought again and then said decisively: 'Then keep out of this yourself at all costs.'

'No word of warning to Julius van Eyck? No hint to be on his guard with Doctor Grant?'

'Certainly not. Except in the Boardroom you shouldn't be seen with him.'

'But—'

'It's entirely unnecessary. I would doubt

if Professor van Eyck lives much longer.'

In contrast to the situation in London which so far was less than deeply penetrated the Brethren's organisation in the low countries was longstanding and widespread, far bigger than a matter of peddling drugs. Nor was the *Compagnie Générale* the only company where their writ ran. At this moment it was the most important but there were others and bigger which in the last resort must bow to the Brethren's nod. And there had always been rackets, as there had almost everywhere. The Brethren had moved in and organised them, cutting out competition, rationalising. Almost always control was scrupulously concealed, but it existed and was steadily growing, through the business world and local government (local government was especially vulnerable) into parliament and national politics.

And on this powerful instrument John Aldo had been playing skilfully. But widespread as by now it was it hadn't yet needed a resident killer and such a one had had to be brought in from America.

Which had extended van Eyck's life by two days.

On arrival the man had been carefully brief-ed, for except in an outbreak of open war between factions, and at the moment Frank Loretto had not been challenged, the Brethren preferred to do their killings discreetly... So Professor van Eyck was old and ailing. He had already had three heart attacks, one of them an actual arrest. There were simple ways of inducing another and a doctor had been at the briefing to show them. A woman came in to cook and clean and the district nurse on alternate days. Otherwise he lived alone and his flat was on the bottom floor. It shouldn't be a difficult job.

The killer had been given keys and had been far too experienced to ask how they had been obtained. John Aldo looked after that sort of detail and his opinion of John Aldo was high.

Now he looked round the Professor's bedroom. Julius van Eyck was dead in his bed. He had a very slight bruise but that would be explicable... Would it be better to tip him onto the floor?... Elderly invalid feels attack coming on; tries to reach the telephone; falls and dies...

The killer pushed the body out of bed. It fell on the floor in an untidy heap.

He looked round the room in a final check. So far it had all gone smoothly and as a professional he mistrusted that. It was easy to make some stupid mistake. He spent five minutes confirming that he had not. Then he let himself out and walked home quietly. It was four in the morning and the streets were deserted.

13

Both Lord George and the Prime Minister used alcohol but with discipline; neither drank before twelve o'clock at the earliest and though both men were watching the clock discreetly the indifferent news hadn't broken their habit. It was far from good but it might have been nothing and that would have troubled both men gravely. Lord George was saying: 'Mr Smith has been doing rather better than well but he isn't quite sure that what he's found is *Belinda.*'

The Prime Minister understood 'Mr Smith' at once. It was a convention to avoid the banal. 'That man I sent to Belgium, you know' would sound like a pretentious spy story and to use his real name would offend sound instincts. So the Executive's operators were always 'Mr Smith'. The Prime Minister asked:

'How far has he got?'

'He thinks he's found *Belinda* but can't be sure. She's lying in a creek called Vlamshaven. It was never much more than a fishing port but now that that trade is dead or dying the place is in effect deserted. It's used as a graveyard for broken-down ships and it's crowded with every sort of rusting hulk. But one of them is being refitted.'

'Not much to go on.'

'Listen a bit. A new engine came in by road and a crane to load it. Expensive for what looks like a write-off. And there's something which looks like a brand new radar. More interestingly, the ship has been wired off. On the land side there's an eight-foot fence and it's regularly patrolled day and night. The patrols appear to carry arms.'

'Name painted out, I suppose?'

'Of course. They'll give her a false registration when she sails. It doesn't much matter what since she's going to be sunk. In British waters. Loaded with death.'

'How big is this suspected *Belinda?*'

'About four hundred tons according to Smith —the size of ship our friend Mathew Cole was working along the Essex coast when that sort of cabotage still paid.'

'Which would carry enough of what we fear—'

194

'I don't dare to think of it.'

'Nor do I.'

There was a silence while both men unwillingly did so. When Lord George spoke again he sounded tentative. 'Can you think of any positive action?'

'Against a ship which may be *Belinda* and may be not? And which as far as we know is still unladen. We may be certain enough about what Loretto is brewing but we haven't a jot of proof to stand up in a court. Action against a ship in a friendly port could easily destroy the vessel (which in passing might only achieve postponement) but would also put us squarely in the wrong. It would be an act of the barest piracy, if not of war.'

'Frogmen slipping in and blowing her up?'

'I thought you said she lay behind a fence. Wouldn't the water be guarded too?' The Prime Minister's brusque manner changed. 'I'm not trying just to put you down. I can see you've thought of something else.'

'I was thinking of diplomacy.'

'Bah! All diplomacy is basically bluff and as such can be called and in this case would be. You could call it a high stakes game of poker and Sir Otto is not the man for that.'

Sir Otto was the ambassador in Brussels. He liked to be called Her Majesty's ambassador.

He was that sort of man.

The Prime Minister was an excellent mimic and his voice dropped into Sir Otto's smoothly plummy Oxbridge, entirely edgeless.

'...Good morning, Minister. It is kind of you to receive me.'

'Not at all. What can I do for you?'

A deliberate but too long-held pause. 'Actually, Minister' (it was one of Sir Otto's favourite words) 'actually I have come with an offer.'

'That is really very kind. What is it?'

'I think it is fairly common ground that your country holds a great deal of nuclear waste.'

The Belgian Minister's voice was ironic. 'If you say it is common knowledge it must be.'

'And that you are finding—shall we say?— some embarrassment in disposing of it with your own resources.'

'What are you trying to tell me, Excellency?' This time the Belgian's voice was sharp.

'We have good facilities for the disposal of all grades of nuclear waste.'

'So?'

'I have come here to offer them.'

'At a price, no doubt.'

'My very dear fellow!' His Excellency sounded deeply offended. 'A matter of money is not for us.'

'I will have it considered. And a very good morning.'

The Prime Minister's voice reverted to his own. He was a fair-minded man and he realised he'd hammed it. 'Perhaps that was a caricature.'

Lord George nodded again. It had been a caricature but not quite an unfair one. The Foreign Secretary had greatly changed but not all the changes had worked through to the very top. One or two Sir Ottos still survived from another age; and unless they did something outrageous (they never did) the easiest way to get rid of them was to let the system excrete them naturally—by age. But it was very bad luck that the Brussels post was held by a man so easy to ridicule. A younger man could have done much more; he could have conveyed not only a lively suspicion but the fact that his country was prepared to defend itself. Not by any overt threats for these were very seldom uttered but a younger man would have left a clear message. Sir Otto would never do that— no, never. Whatever instructions you chose to give him that Belgian Minister would be first a *cher collègue*. One simply didn't get tough in the club.

Lord George nodded for the third time, unhappily. Any move in the strange world of

197

diplomacy was blocked by misfortune and its name was Sir Otto. It was very ill fortune indeed but there it was. For the first time that morning Lord George allowed a smile. The Prime Minister had chosen his own way to tell him but the message had been loud and clear. Lord George abandoned that line for another. 'Anything from Molly Grant?' he asked.

'Only that her Professor has died. A pity, that. What do you make of the death?'

'What do you? He was known to be a dying man and a doctor had seen him the day before. There needn't even be an inquest.'

'It was a remarkably convenient death for Loretto.'

'Suspiciously so,' Lord George said promptly, 'but there's nothing to be gained by saying so. The Belgian police would think we'd gone mad. No, from our point of view that scent is stone cold. I take it you'll recall Molly Grant.'

The Prime Minister's answer was friendly laughter. 'You don't give orders to Molly Grant. I have conveyed to her that she is free to return but she replied that she intended to stay. At her own expense from the date of my message.'

'Whyever is she doing that?'

'She's having a brisk affair with Mario de Var.'

'How on earth do you know?'

'She told me herself.'

It was Lord George's turn for companionable laughter. 'Quite a woman,' he said.

'A gross understatement.' The Prime Minister had been enjoying a joke but returned to the business in hand with a sour grimace. 'So how do we stand on *Belinda?*' he asked. 'We need a positive identification that this ship in Vlamshaven is really the carrier. Given that I would be prepared to act.'

'You would?'

'I must.'

'Then the only line open is still Mr Smith. He has a photograph of what *Belinda* looked like before she was dumped in that creek to rot and he's going to try to get close enough to be sure. But it isn't going to be an easy stalk. I told you they'd put up a fence and they've done more. They've cleared the scrub for fifty yards round it and levelled the dunes. Fifty yards of a sort of *glacis*, wide open to fire from men believed to be armed.'

A telephone on the desk rang shrilly and Lord George frowned. 'I said we were to be left in peace. That must be urgent. May I?'

'Of course.'

Lord George picked the receiver up; his angry frown darkened and he told the Prime

Minister: 'That was the stringer in Ostend and he's breaking all the rules by sending. He's a stringer not an active operator and he may only transmit at fixed times if obliged to. This isn't one of them. He's a steady old file and not easily rattled.'

'He sends in code?'

'A very simple one. The Belgians know he's only a stringer and since he does them no harm they leave him alone. As we leave alone the Belgian stringer here. But if they happen to be listening now they could break his code in a couple of hours. We don't have to break it so we're going to take much less. Shall I keep this line open?'

'Yes, of course.'

Both men sat on in a total silence, the receiver on the desk in front of Lord George. Four long minutes crawled by on their way to eternity, then the receiver on the desk came alive again. The voice in it was the decoder's, English. Lord George picked it up and his patrician face turned to stone. He put it back in its cradle and told the Prime Minister.

'Mr Smith has not been seen or heard from for two days.'

When he kept his appointment for lunch with John Aldo, Charles Russell had been prepared

200

for surprises but not the surprise which in the event he received. Aldo had arrived before him and had employed his advantage by drinking two gins. They had mellowed him but in no way dulled his edge. He rose to greet Charles Russell politely, and when he too had a drink fired his opening shot.

'I would guess that you have placed me accurately.'

'I might not go as far as that but I can see you're not a cut-out Brethren type.'

'You're perfectly correct in that. My family are market gardeners and have been for several generations. The land is on the outskirts of a city which is growing fast so as things have turned out they're paper millionaires. But they don't want to sell and loaf in Florida. Market gardening is their trade; they enjoy it. My father refuses to sell at any price.'

'Admirable sentiments,' Russell said.

'Not entirely for me. I have four brothers, you see, and there wasn't room for me too on the garden. But apart from the land's great capital value the business is well run and prosperous and there was money to send me to college in the east. Where I read law and got a good degree. Quite a well-known firm took me on when I graduated.'

'And then?'

'It took me nearly a year to discover that this eminent firm was an arm of the Brethren. It did little that wasn't strictly legal—that went elsewhere to firms with lesser names—but it was a front for a great deal of Brethren money. As an example it is the nominee owner of the *Compagnie Générale* which I know greatly interests you.'

'How do you know that?'

'I'm Loretto's man of affairs, am I not?'

'And how did that happen?'

'Almost imperceptibly. I found myself meeting Loretto weekly, doing jobs which should have gone to a senior. We built up a very odd relationship. He despises me as the typical college boy; he resents my accent and hates my clothes but he seems to think I've a pretty good brain. After about two years of this he invited me to join him directly.'

'How did you react to that?'

'I jumped at it. You see, he made the position perfectly clear. I wasn't going to be asked to do the chores; I haven't even taken some silly oath. You could call me a sort of senior staff Colonel who doesn't come from the General's own regiment.' Aldo looked at Russell enquiringly. 'But I'm boring you—you will know all this.'

'You're not boring me and I didn't know.'

'But your Security Executive will. It's still a first-class organisation.'

Russell noticed that Aldo hadn't said 'outfit'. He would also have been surprised if he had; he asked 'Was the "still" a regret or a nicely turned compliment?'

'A bit of both.'

'Leave the compliment and explain the regret.'

'I'm in a dilemma.'

'Indeed?'

'A big one. It's widely suspected that I wish to succeed Loretto. I do not. I want out. I've made a good deal of money and I wish to enjoy it.'

'Why shouldn't you?'

'Colonel Russell, you pretend to ignorance. If I walk away from Loretto I won't live long.'

'Yes, I dare say you won't. But why tell me?'

'You could help me.'

'Why should I?'

'We have an interest in common.'

Russell had enjoyed these quickfire exchanges; they conveyed information fast and accurately, something which his time in Whitehall had taught him was a precious rarity. But now it was time to slow things down; this was going to be a tricky hand and he didn't wish to

203

concede a trick fruitlessly. But he would have to lead and he did so carefully:

'We know a good deal about why Loretto came here. Naturally we suspect a lot more.'

Aldo said blandly: 'I'd be surprised if you didn't. I said the Executive were good and I meant it.'

'Thank you again but that's hardly the point.'

Russell had a difficult decision. If his next question were too blunt and uncompromising he might scare John Aldo away for ever; on the other hand he was tired of sparring. He said carefully and even more quietly than usual: 'Are you offering us co-operation?'

'Not directly.'

'Then what *are* you offering?'

Aldo didn't answer directly. 'I said that if I just left Loretto I would know too much and be dead in a week. But if *Loretto* were dead I'd have a chance of survival. There'd be a power struggle for several months and whoever emerged in Loretto's place would have much less motive to put me away. What I knew would be dangerous still but less so to Loretto's successor. I could never go back to the States, of course—that would be cocking a fatal snook—but it might not be worth the new man's while to pursue me into another country.' Aldo leant forward. 'I fancy England. Could you arrange that I live there quietly?'

'It depends what you mean by quietly.'

'What I say. I'd buy a small house and marry and settle down.'

'That we could perhaps arrange.' Charles Russell's mild manner changed abruptly. *'Why should we?'*

'Because your interest in Loretto's death is every bit as strong as mine. If Loretto were to be taken from us before this operation is finished it would automatically go on ice while the power struggle was splitting the Brethren. Very possibly it would be abandoned completely. The new man might not like the smell of it and in any case Loretto's death would signal that the plan had been compromised.'

'I have heard that said before in much the same words. Are you offering to dispose of Loretto?'

'No, again, I'm afraid I am not. That guard of his is a fool but competent and I haven't any training in killing.'

'Then what is the proposition?'

'I must know something first.'

'Go on.'

'Why did you come here with Mario de Var?'

'Loretto had his father murdered and he's a Sicilian nobleman with the code of his kind.

He sees it as a filial duty to kill Frank Loretto if he possibly can. I'm his godfather and fond of him, and sneakingly I rather admire him. He hasn't a hope of getting Loretto and I came with him to prevent any foolishness.'

'You think he hasn't a hope of a killing?'

'Of course he hasn't.' Russell spoke with decision.

'With appropriate respect I disagree. If there were such a chance would you try to dissuade him?'

'I wouldn't read him a lecture on morals.'

Aldo finished his coffee and tapped the table. Instinctively he had lowered his voice. It was unnecessary, a simple reflex. He said in a carefully controlled ellipsis: 'Of course any old night when Loretto swims won't do. It's going to need a getaway car in which I shall be coming too. De Var's good in the water and he won't need to practise, but it's going to require the precisest timing. That timing I could supply on demand.'

'I'll think it over,' Charles Russell said.

Lord George had sat silent for fully five minutes, watching the Prime Minister think. He knew that he liked to do so slowly for he had known him before he had reached that eminence. Lord George was the last of a very

206

large family and Sara, the Prime Minister's wife, was the daughter of his eldest sister. There were only a matter of months between them and many believed they were brother and sister.

They were certainly very alike in habit: both liked their own way and mostly got it, he as a previous Foreign Secretary, she as the wife of a country solicitor who was inching his way up the political ladder. In the matter of faithfulness she had failed him frequently, but this daughter of a great Whig house had done much to oil the political wheels. Moreover she had given him two priceless gifts, the habit of thinking outside the constraints of law and the patrician's talent to act decisively.

So Lord George watched the Prime Minister think deliberately. He would take his time in doing so but when he had reached a decision he would act. There wouldn't be a Royal Commission nor Minutes on some unfruitful file. If he had to put his head on the block the Prime Minister would do so unhesitatingly.

He said at length: 'I spoke of positive identification—of *Belinda*, I mean—before taking any action against her. At times I still catch myself thinking like that—of what a court would consider formal proof—but I've been largely laughed out of it by Sara. Now I have changed my mind about that ship. There are altogether too many coincidences. Contrary to what a judge once said six black rabbits *can* make one black hare.'

'I agree. So what now?'

'You don't mind if I think aloud?'

'Go ahead.'

'There's nothing I can do for the moment—no frogmen or blowing her up from the air. That would be entirely illegal, something I've learnt to discount pretty sharply, but it would leave us without a leg to stand on. But once she sails there are things we can do. We can't sink her in mid-Channel summarily—that would contaminate most of the North Sea—but the moment she gets into British waters I can have her intercepted and I will. We'll put scientists aboard with their instruments and men who know how to handle nuclear waste. Then if she's registering, as Molly Grant tells me she's bound to be, we'll escort her politely back to Belgium. Whereupon I shall blow the whole story.'

'You'll do *what?*'

'I shall call the biggest Press conference ever.'

Lord George whose instincts were strongly for secrecy said uneasily: 'They'll make an enormous meal of it.'

'Precisely what I want them to do. There's something the papers call public opinion, though the term is often misused absurdly. The Left takes it to mean what it thinks itself, or sometimes it's what some pundit says it is. But I don't mean either of those, they're quite spurious. I mean the ordinary unthinking re-action of the ordinary unlettered man. That will be behind me solidly. It was frightened by that Italian ship which sailed round the world from port to port, trying to dump its toxic waste. The suggestion of something far worse than that would put men behind me like nothing else.'

'Another Falklands factor?' Lord George was dry.

'Just so.'

'You have a majority of four at a pinch. Will you call a snap election?'

'Possibly.'

Both men laughed for both were professionals.

Lord George returned to the practicalities. '*Belinda* lies behind wire and I've lost a man spying on her. But she's got to be loaded and that means lorries. The road must go through what's left of Vlamshaven. I wish we had some up-to-date photographs.'

'That can be arranged. There's an exercise

going on with the Dutch Navy and a helicopter can easily stray down the coast a bit. It isn't a full-dress NATO affair so the helicopter won't be there by right. We may be asked to apologise and be sure we shall do so.'

'How long will it take?'

'A few hours if I press it.'

'Please press it.'

'I will.'

The Prime Minister rose. 'Then for the moment that seems to be all.' An afterthought struck him. 'And you'll be sending another man to Ostend?'

'Of course.'

But it hadn't been 'Of course' at all, and as he looked next day at the chopper's photographs Lord George's doubts had been reinforced. Mr Smith's body had not been found: presumably they had taken it into what by now he was sure was *Belinda*. When she sailed they'd weight it and drop it overboard, without benefit of priest or ceremony. Mr Smith had been an experienced operator and such men took time to train and were valuable. He'd been caught on a reconnaissance so *Belinda's* very efficient guardians would know that they were being watched. To send another man would be folly. He would be blown before he even started.

Lord George looked again at the chopper's photographs. They didn't need interpretation since they had been taken from almost roof-top level. Vlamshaven was much as they had told him it was, the ruin of a once-prosperous fishing village. There was something which might still be a shop and something which perhaps was a café but two houses in three were boarded up and the photographs showed not a soul in the streets. They were pictures of a depressing decay but they also showed some-thing else more interesting. A surfaced road did run straight through the middle, down to the port and the waiting *Belinda*. Lorries must use it to reach and load her.

Lord George thought of his 'Of course' again. It hadn't been entirely equivocal. He wouldn't despatch another Smith, not to cer-tain failure and probable death, but he *was* going to send another man and that man was going to be himself.

He hadn't even the ghost of a plan but Col-onel Charles Russell was still in Ostend and Charles Russell's head was as good as ever. In his time he'd been the acknowledged master and now, in retirement, that aura still clung to him. He had the experience that Lord George had not and a better brain.

Lord George was going to Belgium to pick it.

211

There was a service which flew to Ostend directly but it was cramped and flew at inconvenient times. Lord George packed a bag and bade farewell to his wife. She protested but she knew the rules. Then he sent for a taxi and directed it to Heathrow. He knew there were plenty of flights to Brussels where he would find a taxi and drive to Ostend. He would take whichever line flew first. He bought himself a first-class ticket.

To his surprise there was a considerable crowd and presently he saw the reason. A star of the London stage was travelling too and her PR people were making a thing of it. There were Press cameramen and several bouquets and a mêlée of what were presumably admirers. As she left they raised a strangled cheer and Lord George, whose brother worked in advertising, wondered how much they'd been paid to do so.

In the first-class compartment there were only three passengers with the actress and her chief PR man. Lord George, with a sardonic amusement, watched the chief steward fuss and fawn. He had met the lady but didn't accost her. He wasn't in any sense part of her world and it was probable she had wholly forgotten him. In any case he didn't admire her. In politics she was aggressively Left, a position she combined without difficulty with a very high standard of living indeed and a cold and often formidable hauteur.

At Brussels he let her precede him regally, for at the bottom of the flag-draped gangway he could see that the same charade had been mounted. Flashbulbs had begun to pop and there was a little girl in fancy dress (or was it meant to be Flemish peasant costume?) holding a bunch of fading flowers. Lord George waited at the top of the gangway till the scene was almost played out but not quite. There was a single cameraman left at the gangway's foot but the chief steward, who'd paid him scant attention, was standing behind him, coughing discreetly. He wanted to clear his cabin and go home.

Lord George began to move reluctantly and the cameraman took a full-face photograph. He took it on spec but it earned him a front-page spread.

Lord George shrugged resignedly. It was a misfortune but it couldn't be helped.

14

Lord George cleared his bag and walked through the concourse, taking the cab at the head of the rank. The driver took his bag and stowed it, something very unusual in Brussels, and he smiled as he did so, something still rarer. There was a standard fare between the airport and Ostend but mostly drivers would ask for more. This one did not and Lord George was grateful for above all things he detested a haggle. By and large these men were a surly lot and spoke Flemish or at best Bruxelloise but this one had spoken Vallon French. Lord George got in beside him ready to chat. Taxi-drivers, like milkmen and dailies, were a proven source of information. Lord George gave him the name of Charles Russell's hotel and said that he wished to get there quickly but in one piece.

'You speak very good French, sir.'

'I make myself understood. No more.'

'A great deal more.' A pause. 'You learnt it in the war, perhaps?'

'I'm afraid I was too young for the war.'

Lord George looked at the driver reflectively. He was a little older than himself; he asked: 'Were you in the war yourself?'

'They would have called me up if we hadn't been smashed. As it was I went underground. The Resistance.' The driver returned Lord George's inspection. 'The real Resistance,' he added, 'the Communists.'

Lord George knew what he meant exactly. Of all the European Resistances the Belgian had worried the Germans least. Only the Communist hard core had seriously fought. Lord George considered a dangerous question. It might dry this driver up on the spot or conceivably it might lead him on. Lord George decided to take the risk.

'Are you a Communist still?'

'Yes and no. I don't carry a party card any more but I'd still like to see the capitalists hanged. My family were miners, you see. The capitalists shut down the pits and destroyed us.'

'Those pits in the south were almost worked out. The Unions were being difficult.' Lord George laughed mirthlessly. 'Just like England.'

'I don't see it quite like that myself. There's plenty of coal in south Belgium still. They could have opened new pits and made their profit but instead they saw a greater one in nuclear power. And I know in my bones that it's more dangerous than we're told. That's another reason I'm still a communist. With a pretty small 'c' by now perhaps, but I'm convinced and so are most of my friends that the government is covering up.'

'The chance of another Chernobyl?'

'Yes. Your government does that too, no doubt. What it doesn't do is the other shameful thing.'

Lord George didn't ask 'What?' since he didn't need to. The driver was letting his hair down happily, talking with something approaching relief.

'Any nuclear power means nuclear waste. In most other countries they deal with that properly but here it's got hopelessly out of hand. No doubt we have places to deal with some of it but production hasn't been geared to fit them. There's an enormous surplus still undisposed of.'

'May I ask where you got all this?'

'It's common knowledge.'

'Common gossip, you mean?' There was a hint of acidity.

But the driver was in no way offended; he was enjoying his chat with this intelligent Englishman. 'I can do a little better than that.

216

I take a Left-wing newspaper and a month ago it ran an article. It was off the streets next morning for a week. When it returned it talked about some printing trouble. Capitalist printers, you see, so there you were. But it never said another word about a problem which keeps me awake at night.'

'So what do you think is going to happen?'

Without lifting his hands from the wheel the driver shrugged. 'I cannot even guess how they'll do it but get rid of that deadly stuff they must. Someone's going to make a great fortune.'

They had arrived at the Royal George in Ostend and Lord George paid the driver off with a generous tip. To his astonishment the driver declined it. 'It's been a pleasure to talk as we have. I dare not often.'

'You really mean dare not?'

'Look what happened to my daily paper.'

Lord George booked a room and enquired for Doctor Molly Grant. The reception clerk rang her room and said: 'She asks you to go up at once.'

Lord George went up in the lift and knocked on the door. A stranger opened it wide and he saw the room. Charles Russell and Molly Grant had risen. 'George,' she said, 'what a pleasant surprise. You know everybody except

217

Mario.' She waved a hand at Mario de Var. 'Baron Mario de Var,' she said.

Lord George bowed politely and Mario clicked.

'I talked about a pleasant surprise but my guess is that you've come with bad news. So let's sit down and get it over.'

Lord George explained the position precisely. At the end he looked at Russell. 'You first, please.'

'If you wish.' Charles Russell had done his thinking as Lord George talked. 'So we don't have any more doubts on *Belinda*. The Prime Minister is prepared to act, a decision he was bound to make, but only in waters unquestionably British. That is going to need pretty careful arrangements—Royal Navy ships and scientists on them. It's a question of timing and I don't see an answer. He can hardly mount a standing patrol at Miller's Sound.'

'I've a theatrical answer but not a practical.' Lord George produced the strayed helicopter's photographs and passed them round. 'That's the ruined village of Vlamshaven and *Belinda* lies just below her in the creek. We know that she's almost ready to sail but before she does she has got to be loaded. She can only be reached by road, which means lorries. And the road runs straight through what's left of Vlam-shaven.'

No one had spoken though all had understood. Finally Charles Russell said softly: 'And you've lost a Mr Smith already.' He raised his eyebrows in silent enquiry but Lord George shook his handsome head emphatically. Charles Russell said: 'I wouldn't have either.'

'Thank you.'

The exchange had been in its own way coded, one between men of the same profession. Mario wasn't quite sure he had followed it. 'If I may ask a question, sir?'

'Go ahead.'

'The essential we need to know is when she loads. A man in the village could tell us that. And the village is in effect a ruin.'

'But almost certainly patrolled at night.'

Mario said: 'I'm good at night.'

There was an astonished silence till Russell broke it, saying with a clear hint of impatience, a man who was being pushed too far: 'I thought you came here to kill Loretto.'

'I did. And you came too to police me discreetly, to see that I took no outrageous chances. So far I've had no chance of any sort and it begins to look as though I never shall. But if I can't kill him I can do him an injury and finding out when the *Belinda* sails would be that.'

There was a feeling of two men at odds and Lord George came in smoothly to heal the breach. 'That would certainly set Loretto back. We should know where we stood and could time it accordingly. But spying at night in enemy territory needs training and you haven't had it.'

Mario looked at Russell in silent appeal. It was a message again and Charles Russell read it. He had been irritated but remained fair-minded. 'He said he was good at night,' he said, 'and I've personal reason to know he was telling the truth.'

Lord George inclined his head but wasn't convinced. 'The patrol or patrols will be arm-ed to the teeth.'

'He carries a knife. A bloody great knife.' It was Molly Grant.

'Not decisive against a man with a pistol.'

'I dare say you could find him that.'

Mario held a hand up quickly. 'I shan't take a knife and I shan't take a pistol. Killing with a knife you can never be sure—sure that the man won't cry out before he dies. And even silenced pistols make some noise. If I have to kill I shall have to kill silently or they'll take the village to pieces to find me. When I shan't be able to give you any news.'

'And how do you propose to kill silently?'

Mario took something from his pocket and dangled it. Charles Russell drew his breath in sharply for he had seen this weapon used by commandos in war. Once the rachet was on the victim was dead. It was an unpleasant death but one totally silent. 'That's a horrible thing,' Russell said.

'I know. But you forget that I come from a horrible people.' The Baron Mario de Var stood up. 'And now,' he said, 'I shall buy a bicycle.'

Molly Grant had once praised her God that Mario was not what she called a sensitive but he had the cool realism of the upper class and he could see that Charles Russell, even more so Lord George, were in a position which at best was anomalous. Things might work out and very possibly would so they'd be obliged to admit that they knew his intention but would be grateful to add, with their hands on their hearts, that they knew nothing of his actual plan.

This he therefore made alone. A road map told him the distance to Vlamshaven and he cycled a similar distance, timing it. He memorised the photographs carefully. If the village was also patrolled by day that was a matter which didn't concern him, but the night patrol would come on at dusk and the change would be the best time to slip in.

This evening he was pedalling strongly, looking at his watch as he rode and watching the fading light intently. He didn't intend to ride into Vlamshaven: he would hide his bicycle in the scrub which surrounded it and try to get in through a tangled back garden.

He had chosen his house with a deliberate care for it was the tallest in the village by a storey. The attic, if he could reach the attic, commanded a view of the creek and *Belinda* and another window looked east along the road. A third looked down on the village street.

He hid his bicycle in a thicket of scrub and climbed over the low brick wall of the garden. By now it was a minor jungle but Mario made his way through it confidently, sure-footed and entirely silent. He knew that the house was boarded up but also that it had been so for some time. The shutters would be loose and rotten and the only danger in forcing one would be that of making a noise in doing so.

In the event he didn't have to use force for one of the crumbling boardings had fallen. He slipped through the gaping window into the house. He had brought a torch but used it sparingly. The floor was littered by fallen plaster and rats ran away as the torch's light caught them, their rodent eyes gleaming with malice in the beam. He picked his way through the house to the staircase and stopped dead.

The staircase was a total ruin. One tread in two had fallen away and the others were about to do the same. To attempt it would be utter folly. He tried the banister but it rocked in his hand.

He stood back and considered, using the torch again since he must. The house had been a biggish one, perhaps the harbour-master's in the days of prosperity, and the staircase was of a fashion to suit it, doubling back on itself at a midway landing. When he stood underneath it he couldn't reach it but with one of the fallen treads in his hand he could. With this he prodded the floorboards suspiciously. They creaked but at one point they didn't give. He measured the distance, his arms held above him. He was three feet short of the boards above his head: he would have to make a running jump. The bannister on the landing had fallen, there was no obstacle if he caught and the landing held.

He stood back and considered the chances dispassionately. The jump would increase the strain as his weight fell, and apart from any question of injury the whole thing could come crashing down and betray him. But the alternative was to admit defeat, to find another house and try again. But no other house had this attic eyrie and a good field of vision was essential to his purpose.

Finally Mario ran and jumped, falling short by what he guessed was inches. Methodically he cleared the floor to the further wall. This gave him an extra two strides and he jumped again. This time he caught and for a second hung motionless. The woodwork had groaned but it hadn't fallen. Then his strong swimmer's arms pulled him up to the landing.

He lay for a moment, catching his breath, sweating and not wholly from effort. Above him lay the rest of the stairs. They were in much better shape than those below but they were suspect still and he tackled them cautiously, not walking but crawling, spreading his weight. At their head was another landing with bedroom doors. They were still on their hinges and Mario felt easier. He opened one and there it was, the trap-door to the loft above and a ladder. It had been held up by a rope which had long since rotted. Now it was in position invitingly. Mario saw that it was made of steel.

He went up it quickly, for the first time almost confident, but he still crawled to the window which overlooked the street below.

The shop, if there was one, he couldn't see but he was opposite the little bar.

The night was warm and on the pavement in front of it a little huddle of men and women sat drinking bock. All were elderly and one or two seedy, the detritus of this run-down community, too old or too poor to escape from its decay. A single man sat apart from them and sometimes they would glance at him nervously. An animal would have picked up the scent of fear.

Presently a second man walked deliberately up from the creek and *Belinda*. He nodded briefly to the first and took his place. When he had done so he called to the *patron*, who looked resentful but too scared to protest. He put out the overhead light and locked the bar. The old people dispersed and the man from the creek got up and was lost in the dark.

For two nights nothing of interest happened and Mario used them to learn the night-patrol's routine, watching from each window in turn, following the man's torch as he flashed it over the broken buildings. He used it without restraint; he was the boss. Satisfied, he would search one house, a different one on each of two nights. Then he would disappear for some hours. Presumably he had a hide of his own, probably with a camp bed to nap on, but just before dawn he would always appear again, do ing his rounds till relieved at dawn.

The third night there was a crisis and it came unexpectedly. As far as Mario had been able to tell the patrol's choice of a house to search was something which he made at random and tonight he had chosen the wreck which hid Mario. Mario could hear him forcing the front door, and once inside he would immediately be suspicious. For Mario hadn't risked further climbing: instead he had brought a rope with a grapnel, throwing it direct to the second floor.

That was still in place to betray his presence.

He heard the man below him exclaim and at the same time the rumble of distant lorries. The arc lights beyond *Belinda* came on. Instinct told him the hanging rope had tautened.

…So everything's going to happen at once.

On the floor below the three-windowed attic the patrol was searching the bedrooms carefully. He was making a good deal of noise in doing so but hadn't a reason to care for that. The rumble of the approaching lorries was now a roar.

The patrol came last to the room with the steel ladder to the loft. He began to climb.

Mario knelt at the trapdoor's mouth. The arcs from *Belinda* threw strips of light but patches of dappled shadow too and in one of these he waited tensely. The patrol would climb with his face away from him.

The head came up above the floorboards, the neck unprotected, the perfect target. Mario made no mistake with the garotte. He pulled sharply and the ratchet clicked wickedly. A pistol clattered down the steel ladder, then the night patrol fell down behind it.

Mario followed him, watching unhappily. The man was tearing at the wire round his neck, helpless to release its murderous grip. Finally he fell down and began to writhe. Mario made himself watch till his victim was dead.

He stepped back from the body, surprised he was shivering, torn by emotions he hadn't expected. He had killed before, at the airstrip, and more than one man. But they had been bringing in drugs to destroy his people, to leave a legacy of growing evil which more powerful countries had never defeated. He had hated them and had killed with gusto; he had had personal motive and tonight he had had none. He had killed this Belgian (was he a Belgian? He might have been anything) a hireling against whom he'd had nothing. In a private sense he felt diminished.

He reined his thinking sharply; he had done what he must. He had been willing to do Frank

Loretto an injury; he hadn't been ordered to spy, he had volunteered. He had killed because he must get back with his news and dead himself he couldn't have done so. Mario de Var had done his duty.

Duty! It was no doubt admirable but it was something in the mind, almost abstract. So three cheers for duty and tra-la-la. But duty didn't grip the viscera, as natural as the urge to defecate, and Mario was a visceral man.

The lorries were passing the house in a stream and Mario went to the window to watch them. Their headlights were on and it was easy to count them. Three had already gone past but were visible and he counted seventeen more behind them. They were eight-wheelers, high-sided, the sort which contractors used for hardcore. But tonight they weren't loaded with hardcore or aggregates: they were loaded with what looked like petrol drums. For a moment the column checked and Mario could count again. Each lorry held twenty-four drums packed tightly.

So now he must get back to Charles Russell. He went down his rope and shook the grapnel loose. He wound the rope round his waist as he'd brought it, under his coat. He found his bicycle and rode hard to Ostend.

Lord George was in a familiar dilemma, not one about what to do but of the means. He seldom read what were condescendingly called spy stories but when he did he read with scepticism. They were, he remembered now, of two kinds. In the first the spy did his business straightforwardly but in the second he was filled with self-doubt and *angst*. Intellectual critics preferred the latter: Lord George did not. If he wished to know more of the nature of man there were competent books which told it straight, or he could go to the psychologist (he would freeze you if you called him a psychiatrist) who sat on the Executive's Board.

But all these books had one thing in common: they were cagey about communications. Sometimes there was pseudotechnical name-dropping about microdots or drops or carriers but none of these gave a hint of guidance on the position in which he found himself now. He was head of the Security Executive and he must speak to his Prime Minister urgently.

He considered his choices, shaking his head. He had a normal, rather low-grade stringer, but he was almost certainly monitored. Alternatively he could drive to Brussels and a man who had once been the Foreign Secretary had the clout to make reluctant diplomats act. But that would waste essential time and had another even more serious drawback. Any message sent by the Brussels embassy wouldn't reach the Prime Minister's ear directly. It would go first to somebody's desk in the Foreign Office and it was Lord George's firm and established opinion, one which he was prepared to defend, that in any matter of naked crisis the less the FO knew the better.

Finally he made up his mind: he'd have to telephone and accept the risk. In England the line was completely secure but at this end it might well be tapped. Sheer urgency overruled that decisively.

Lord George picked up the telephone and dialled a number in England. It was one little known and infrequently used. Somewhere along the line he heard a hum. That would be the scrambler cutting in. A surprised voice said: 'Who's that?'

'Good morning, Clement. It's me here, George.'

The Christian names were entirely exceptional. They said better than any words: 'This is serious.'

'Where are you?'

'In Ostend.'

'You went yourself instead of sending another man?'

It was an otiose question, one asked to gain

time to think. Lord George said simply: 'Yes' and waited.

'And obviously you have news.'

Lord George gave it into a total silence. At the end the Prime Minister asked: 'Is that all?' He had finished his thinking and recovered his poise. 'Then one or two questions, please.'

'I'll try.'

'You say twenty lorries with twenty-four barrels each. Have you spoken to Molly Grant?'

'Of course.'

'And what does she say?'

'She said that when that lot started to go it would contaminate much more than East Anglia. It would reach into the Midlands at least.'

'And you say they've cut down *Belinda's* masts. We agreed that would be so we shouldn't spot her before the seawater got at those drums and rotted them. And what did she say about that?'

'She gave it about two months before the first major leak. After that the graph would go up like a steeple.'

'Very well,' the Prime Minister said, 'I'll pull the switch.'

'You've laid the circuits?'

'Of course I have.' There was a hint of irritation now. 'And in the process learnt some facts I didn't know. Take the men with scrambled eggs on their hats.'

'The Admirals demurred?'

'They did not. They grinned like cats and one even laughed. They thought of the whole desperate thing as a sort of traditional dream come true...Foreign ship boarded by force if necessary and escorted back to Belgium by armed ratings...' The Prime Minister's sigh was clearly audible. 'There's something odd about naval officers. The more senior they become the more childlike. That doesn't seem to happen with soldiers or airmen. But I haven't a doubt they'll act most efficiently.'

'And the scientists, the men in long white coats?'

'The scientists took it much more seriously. They had the knowledge to be severely frightened and they were. But they'll go aboard with their instruments and cameras and they'll give us an unanswerable case.'

'Which you'll then make public?'

'Yes, I told you. Public opinion will be squarely behind me and I once told you too what I meant by that. I don't mean the media and certainly not the United Nations. I mean ordinary men and women all over the West. Not just the Greens but the whole baying pack of them. *Belinda's* load could bring down a government. But it won't. I shall have taken action and been seen to have done so. To put it crudely I'll be on the pig's back.' The Prime Minister's normal cool manner returned. 'Meanwhile, as I said, I must pull that switch. My very sincerest thanks.'

'Not at all.'

Lord George put down the telephone and thought. His Whig genes approved the Prime Minister's *realpolitik*. He had known and mistrusted two other Prime Ministers and both of them would have found a fudge. This one, on the other hand, was going for the outright kill and if that were to his advantage too he wouldn't disdain to pick up his bonus. Politics were not for the scrupulous.

But there was going to be a price to pay, an enormous international rumpus. The Prime Minister knew it but was ready to let the storm blow itself out. Lord George, who'd been a Foreign Secretary, wondered if he realised the storm's extent. And Belgium was an ally in NATO. Not one of importance but still an ally. The Lords of NATO would not be pleased.

How different it would all have been if that godson of Russell had killed Frank Loretto! The sequence of events had been unanimously agreed. There would be an interregnum in the Brethren's monarchy and until a new king had fought his way to the throne this foray into nuclear waste, something quite new and quite untested, the late king's brainchild and not approved everywhere, would be frozen and perhaps even killed...No armed British seamen boarding a Belgian ship, no enormous stone in diplomacy's petty pond.

But de Var had had no chance in hell. The whole idea had been a castle in Spain.

Lord George corrected himself. A castle in Sicily.

Mario and Molly had gone swimming that evening and there they had seen Loretto and his guard. They had seen them before for they too came regularly, but each pair ignored the other's presence. Except that Aldo had once made Molly a tiny bow.

Molly and Mario had finished their swimming and were sitting in towelling, watching the others. The pool wasn't crowded and Loretto was diving. He was using the high board and making a show of it, raising his arms and lowering them ritually, throwing back his head and balancing. Then he ran along the board and jumped. He went in with very little splash.

Mario said: 'He's good but not that good. In the water he'd be very vulnerable.'

'Vulnerable to what?'

'To me.'

'Don't be a bloody fool,' Molly said. She said it with exasperation for she had hoped that he'd been weaned into sense. 'You've done your share of damage already. Vlamshaven and that ship, I mean.' She ended a little weakly. 'All that.'

'But I came here to kill him.'

'Well, you won't do it here in this pool and leave alive. That guard of his would get you first time.'

He said on a note of what was almost reflection: 'There was a time when my own life would not have concerned me.' He gave her a look which she read with sharp pleasure. 'But now I'm rather ashamed that it does.'

'I've been waiting to hear you say that for some time.'

15

The guard was saying to Aldo rudely: 'The boss wants to see you and make it quick.' Aldo knew that this dangerous oaf despised him, and for exactly the reasons Loretto did, but up to this morning he had mostly concealed it. That he was now openly offensive was more than a casual change: it was ominous. The guard was not an intelligent man but he had an animal's sense of the air around him. John Aldo was out of favour increasingly. It was perfectly safe to show his contempt for him.

Aldo said he would come at once but did not: instead he took five minutes to think. His relationship with Frank Loretto had always been one of mutual convenience and he had realised that it was falling apart. There had been a dozen small things but one very serious. Loretto had ordered Molly Grant to be mugged without even informing the man paid to counsel him. He had never done that before and it was bad.

Loretto received him with surprising courtesy and in a language which Aldo had not expected. For apart from his debased Sicilian Frank Loretto was in effect bilingual since he could speak two sorts of American fluently. One was the gutter language of his youth, the other a speech which was socially acceptable. The former he still cherished fiercely: it was part of the macho image he cultivated, the Uh-huhs and grunts and four letter words, and these he still affected fondly.

The second speech he had acquired by *force majeure*. His wife had had powerful social ambitions and in the circles in which she wished to move her husband's speech was quite unacceptable. So she had sent him to an elocutionist, one who would also improve a client's vocabulary. He had protested furiously, she was stealing his manhood, but finally he had given in. In the new image which the Brethren cultivated the family was all-important. The days of the brassy floozie had gone. A discreet mistress might be kept discreetly but a broken family was wholly taboo, even a public rift between husband and wife. So Loretto, though much offended, had given in.

He was using his new speech this morning, talking to Aldo. John Aldo took it as a very bad omen, for normally he barked and brayed at him, anxious to emphasise who was the boss, seeking to humiliate a servant he valued but despised. He was saying mildly: 'Things haven't been going as well as they might.'

John Aldo mistrusted the mildness deeply for he had seen Frank Loretto use it on other men. The technique was to be gently reasonable, cat watching its off-guard prey till the final pounce. He asked:

'In what way?'

'Take Miss Grant, then, to start with. We didn't expect to find her here.'

'She was sent to soften Professor van Eyck. I'm confident he gave little away and in any case he's no longer with us.'

'That was well done,' Loretto said, and Aldo became more uneasy than ever. This too was a part of Loretto's technique, praise where it was due, then the kill. But he was talking on, still overtly civilised.

'And what about de Var and Russell? Why are they here at the same time we are?'

'De Var's motive, I should have thought, was obvious. He has a score to settle and has come here to settle it. Of course he has no hope of doing so.'

'And Colonel Russell?'

'Is Mario's godfather and known to be fond of him. He has come here to prevent any foolishness.'

'But he was head of the British secret service.'

'And retired from that now for several years. He hasn't the machine to harm us.'

'Then what do you make of this, my friend?' Loretto produced a newspaper, laying it on the table, front page up. It wasn't one of the major newspapers but a tabloid with a big circulation. The freelance photographer had placed his random shot of Lord George and the banner above it was unequivocal:

HEAD OF BRITISH SECURITY SLIPS INTO BELGIUM

Loretto was still speaking his second language but his manner had begun to harden.

'Did you know about this?'

'No, I did not.' Aldo's voice was casual still but he realised that he had suffered a wound. A man had been caught spying on *Belinda* and they might well decide to send another. He had thought of that. But there were a score of ways of entering Belgium and it was impossible to watch them all even if the man's identity had been known. As to Lord George that hadn't occurred to him. If it had he wouldn't have taken it seriously and in any case there were equal difficulties. But Loretto was going to exploit it ruthlessly. John Aldo was on the defensive and knew it.

Frank Loretto's voice had acquired an edge. 'I pay you to be my ears and eyes.'

'I'll get after it at once.'

'There is no need, I've already looked after it. We have several people here who aren't fools and one of them, on my orders, has traced Lord George. He has gone to the same hotel as the other three.'

Bad, Aldo thought, very bad indeed. I'm a fish on a line and he's playing me—enjoying it. When the gaff comes out I'll be as dead as a salmon. But perhaps it was worth one more effort before the strike.

'The other three are already tailed. I'll arrange for Lord George to be covered too.'

'And you think that's enough?'

'Against what?'

'I'll tell you.' The manner was still quietly reasonable but the steel was out and glinting dangerously. 'Belinda is sailing in a matter of hours. She would have gone already but for some trouble with the masts. So here we are within hours of success and the head of the British Dirty Tricks joins up with three others already suspect.'

'There simply isn't time for dirty tricks.' It was spoken with confidence for Aldo felt confident.

'Is that your considered opinion?'

'It is.'

'It isn't mine.'

John Aldo looked at Loretto sharply. He was still speaking the language of civilised men but he had straightened in his chair and he wasn't smiling. The hook was in now and being twisted sadistically. Loretto said again: 'It isn't mine.'

'Then what do you want me to do?' It was bound to come some time so he might as well have it now.

'I want all four of them put where they cannot harm us.'

'And how do I do that?'

Loretto told him.

'It's utter madness.'

'You are refusing?'

'Yes.'

'Then you're walking dead.'

Walking dead, Aldo thought, as he left Frank Loretto. He had heard Mario use the same phrase in Sicily. The contexts had been very different but in both they had been entirely accurate.

When Aldo had gone Frank Loretto laughed. He understood John Aldo perfectly. He was a first-class organiser, well worth his money, and Loretto's eyes and ears into different worlds.

But he had never quite accepted the Brethren's creed. In a matter like this he would still have scruples and any scruple made him finally useless. Mass killings had latterly gone out of fashion but now that they were back again Aldo had predictably flinched. His usefulness was outweighed: he'd have to go.

Meanwhile he must arrange this matter himself.

He summoned his guard and they took a taxi, driving to a house in the suburbs. It belonged to a man in Loretto's network, not a pusher but a trusted executive. He listened to Loretto and nodded. 'The explosive,' he said, 'will be perfectly simple but the timing device may be much more difficult.' In fact it would be just as easy but he was a businessman trying to push his price up. They settled in the end for two hundred grand. Loretto wrote an American cheque and the Belgian accepted it perfectly happily. He understood Mr Frank Loretto as Loretto understood John Aldo. Loretto was a world-class criminal and in minor matters completely untrustworthy. But he wouldn't dream of giving the Belgian a bouncing cheque. To do so would be a loss of face and Loretto valued face very highly.

John Aldo went to his room and locked the

door. The action was the purest reflex for he didn't expect immediate action. Nevertheless he had recognised crisis.

He had expected it for some months but had hoped against hope. Perhaps they might even let him go quietly provided he agreed to leave the United States. Which is what he had wished to do in any case. A very big perhaps no doubt, but conceivable if he played his cards right. And now he had no cards to play: it was confrontation, simple and stark. Frank Loretto had forced the occasion deliberately.

And he had done so with his usual cunning. He, Aldo, was here in the same hotel with a bodyguard who would obey orders blindly. They probably wouldn't kill him in Belgium—the complications would be too great and too numerous. No, they would fly him back to the States on a stretcher... Some drug. With the sort of money Loretto commanded there'd be a doctor to provide the cover. And it was no good trying to run in Belgium. For one thing he'd be tagged by the bodyguard and for another he had nowhere to run. He had contacts in Belgium but they were all of them Loretto's men. He hadn't a private friend of any kind.

He thought with regret of Colonel Charles Russell but shook his head. He had made his approach but had heard no more. 'I'll think it over,' Charles Russell had said, and Aldo knew enough of such men to read this as a courteous No. Killing Loretto would certainly serve Russell's ends; it would give him time at the least and very possibly more. But killing him in a public bath, or rather letting Mario kill him, called for skilled and detailed organisation. He remembered he'd offered 'precisest timing' but this hadn't been enough for a cool old pro. He should have offered some concrete plan in detail, the getaway car and all the logistics. But he hadn't dared to rush his fences.

And now he'd heard nothing from Russell and never would.

The reason, he decided, was obvious. Motive, or rather a motive's absence. Mario de Var had a motive which tore his guts but Russell was a thinking animal. No doubt he would wish to serve his country but he would have considered the proposition calmly and decided that it wasn't a good risk. Rightly, John Aldo conceded—quite rightly. He was retired and in a foreign country; he no longer had a machine behind him. Above all he had no personal motive, something of duty but nothing of unthinking anger, of Mario de Var's blind fury which killed thought.

Aldo went out and bought a bottle of whisky, noticing that the bodyguard tailed him. He didn't interfere but followed him back. Aldo went to his room and drank a third of the whisky. There was no particular reason not to.

The four of them were dining at the Chopin again, Lord George, Charles Russell, Molly Grant and Mario de Var. All four were gay though for different reasons. Lord George had told Russell the Prime Minister's decision, that he would tell the whole truth and tell it publicly, leaving a worldwide sense of outrage to carry him through the political crisis which would result. The plan was bold but sound and it would work. Russell had agreed that it probably would, but he had a longer experience than Lord George had yet gathered, and in the world of international politics events weren't always predictable logically. It was the best solution possible as things stood but by no means the best possible solution. That would have been Frank Loretto's death but he hadn't died and he wasn't going to. Nevertheless Charles Russell drank happily. There was going to be an enormous rumpus but *Belinda* wouldn't be sunk in Miller's Sound.

Mario and Molly Grant had other and better

reasons for gaiety.

The restaurant was as crowded as ever and crowded with its usual customers, prosperous upper-middle class customers who liked good food and ate it with gusto. Except for one couple which stood out prominently. They were too fashionably dressed for the Chopin's ambience, more at home in the slick restaurant of the Grand. Moreover they were talking French, whereas the language of the homely Chopin was Flemish or as often English. They had given Charles Russell's table a hard look, then gone back to their conversation in Belgian French. The woman had an outsize handbag and Russell noticed that she never used it. She left it on the floor by her side. She was wearing quite heavy make-up and it needed repair.

Odd, Russell thought, and an alarm bell rang sharply. When the *patron* came up to chat politely he asked him, keeping it wholly casual, who that rather unusual couple were. The *patron* shrugged; he had never seen them before and his manner conveyed rather better than words that if he never saw them again he could bear it. They weren't the sort his establishment catered for.

The strangers finished first, paid their bill and got up. The woman left her bag behind her. She had footed it under the table as she rose but an attentive waiter saw it and picked it up.

Charles Russell was on his feet as fast as a boy. The *patron* had opened the restaurant's door, bowing the strangers out with ceremony. Russell took the bag from the waiter and threw it into the street in a single swing.

There was an explosion, then a second of silence, broken by uproar inside the restaurant. The windows had been blown in by the blast and the *patron* at the door knocked flat. He was picking himself up, shocked but whole. The broken window had meant flying glass and several diners were cut and bleeding. Women were screaming and men swearing pointlessly.

Charles Russell looked round the restaurant coolly. Nobody was going to die.

He strode back to his table and gave crisp, calm orders.

'None of us is a doctor. Let's go.'

Lord George said. 'But the police—'

'The police can hold us as material witnesses and they can do that for an indefinite time. And that's the very last thing I want to happen.'

'What are you going to do?'

'You'll see.'

247

They followed him into the street like obedient sheep. By the grace of the local saints on their own ground the street at the time had been almost deserted. Only two bodies lay huddled, the strangers, but in the distance a police siren was clamouring and people were converging from both sides. Russell led his group towards the Royal George at a brisk walk.

'I don't like this running away,' Lord George said.

'We're not running.'

'Don't quibble. We've a duty—'

'Hell! If we stay and talk we'll bitch the whole thing.'

'What thing?'

Russell said again: 'You'll see.' The strongest of all emotions gripped him, one beyond thought and a world from reason. He hadn't expected to feel it again.

Colonel Charles Russell was blind battle-angry.

16

At the Royal George the lift wasn't working but Russell had them upstairs at a creditable double, making by unspoken consent for the privacy of Molly Grant's room. Inside he asked: 'May I use your telephone?' Bombings in a public place he had always considered the ultimate savagery, indiscriminate murder and an evil in a class of its own. Frank Loretto was a criminal engaged in an unprecedented crime but so far he hadn't behaved like a terrorist. To Charles Russell that had changed the whole picture. But though he was in a cold controlled rage he was speaking rather more softly than usual. Molly hadn't heard him the first time so he said again: 'May I use your telephone, please?'

She nodded but asked: 'Do you want to talk privately?'

'On the contrary I want you to hear every word.'

'Then you'd better hold the receiver well out.' Her eyes were shining with sharp excitement but she was almost as collected as Russell.

'There's an extension in the bedroom and Mario and I will use that. You and George take this one here.'

Russell waited till they had reached the bedroom, then picked up the telephone and rang the Grand hotel. Lord George had pulled up a chair beside him.

'I want to speak to a Mr John Aldo.' Charles Russell put the receiver between them.

'He's in his room, sir, indisposed.'

'If you give him my name I think he will speak with me.' Charles Russell gave his name and waited.

A slightly unsteady voice asked: 'Really Colonel Russell?'

'Yes. Have you been drinking?'

'A little, sir.'

'Are you understanding me?'

'Perfectly.'

'Then have you heard what happened tonight at the Chopin?' He was taking it entirely for granted that Aldo had had no hand in the bombing. Arranging a discreet killing by the way was probably a part of his duties, especially when his master, Loretto, was playing on another side's ground, but the thought had never crossed Russell's mind that John Aldo would agree to a massacre. Charles Russell was an experienced judge of men. Mass murder and maiming were not in John Aldo's book of words.

Who was saying now: 'Yes, there's been a flash on the box. Just what happened—no details.'

'Did you know it was going to happen?'

'Yes, I did. In fact I was told to arrange it.'

'You refused?'

'I said it was mad.'

'Awkward for you,' Charles Russell said.

'Very awkward. I was followed when I went out for a whisky and now they've locked me up in my room. They're feeding me and watering me but the first chance of shutting my mouth they'll take.' John Aldo had sobered remarkably quickly and was speaking perfectly normally now.

'Do you think we're being listened to?'

'No. There hasn't been time to arrange a bug and Loretto and that hood of his will be eating in the restaurant downstairs. After that they're going swimming as usual.'

'You're sure of that?'

'I heard them say so.'

'Can you go too?'

'It isn't a question of "can"—they'll take me. Like it or not they'll take me with them. They can't take the risk that I somehow break

251

away. A mutinous servant with far too much knowledge.'

Charles Russell had been speaking urgently; now he became as bland as a bishop. 'You remember we had a discussion once? You offered, well, co-operation.'

'I realise I didn't offer enough.'

'You could tonight if you wish to do so. You could neutralise Loretto's guard while Mario de Var kills Loretto.'

'You think that's on.'

'With a bit of luck.'

'That oaf's armed,' Aldo said, 'and I am not.'

'The last thing I want is shooting in public. Do you know if that guard can swim?'

'Not a stroke.'

'So much the better. He'll be keeping you by his side no doubt, but his attention will be on Frank Loretto. When I raise my hand you push him in.'

'As simple as that?'

'Simple but to us essential.'

There was a silence while John Aldo thought and when he spoke it was a little uncertainly. 'And for that you'll help me to get away from them?'

'I'll do what I can. I cannot make extravagant promises but there will have to be a car to escape in and in that car there'll be room for you. I can guarantee your arrival in England but after that it's not for me. I'm delighted to say that I'm not the Home Secretary.'

'I'll do it,' John Aldo said.

'And the timing?'

'They'll just have finished eating. Give yourselves twenty minutes—no more.'

'Then I'll hope to see you in twenty minutes.'

Charles Russell put the receiver back and beside him Lord George's smile was complaisant. Throughout these exchanges he hadn't spoken; he hadn't had any reason to do so. He was head of the Security Executive but he was out of his manor, without a machine. Charles Russell, on the other hand, had something better than any machine; he had an experienced eye for the least oppportunity and the skill and flair to turn it to fruitful use.

And there was another good reason for non-interference for Lord George was now seeing what once he had thought. Charles Russell was an Anglo-Irishman, a people with a character of their own. They boasted, sometimes quite close to truthfully, that they had always married among themselves, that they hadn't a drop of Celtic blood, but as the centuries had slipped sleepily by they had become more Irish

253

than the Irish themselves. They could certainly be as bloody-minded. They drew their own
Pale of what was civilised conduct and Loretto
had committed an act of terrorism. That was
the ultimate evil, anathema. As a result there
were now two vendettists not one, and one of
them a good commander.

It was a couple of minutes before Mario and
Molly Grant returned. On the telephone Charles Russell had said: 'While Mario de Var kills
Loretto.' He'd had a shadow of doubt that
Mario would do so but to suggest a method he
would have thought an impertinence. So give
them a couple of minutes to decide.

When she came back Molly Grant looked
radiant. When she'd left she'd been excited and
tense; now she looked several years younger
and relaxed. She was a physicist but first a
woman, and Russell was far too sane and
modest to suppose that he could read a
woman's mind; but he had flashes of feminine
intuition and one of these told him why Molly
was happy. She had decided to settle for Mario
de Var and Mario would be much easier to live
with if he had paid his debt to his father's
ghost. Now she said without preamble: 'It
seems to us there are two loose ends.'

'Tell us,' Russell said.

'First the car. We shall certainly need one to get away in.'

'I was going to call a taxi and highjack it later. Naturally we'd make it up to the driver.'

'Unnecessarily complicated. We'll take mine. It belongs to a hire company and I'm not a thief so wherever we dump it I'll send them a cheque.'

Lord George intervened at last. 'You may leave that to us. Where is your car?'

'In the square outside.'

'That's settled, then. And the other point?'

'Clothes.'

Both men said together: 'Clothes?'

'Yes, clothes. Mario proposes to join Loretto in his little swim. He can't arrive in swimming trunks. That would attract attention at once and the attendants don't like it since it cheats them of their tips. So he'll have to change at the pool in the ordinary way. But there won't be time to go down for his clothes again and he can't drive to wherever we're going half-naked. So I'm packing a suitcase and taking an overcoat. Give me four minutes.' She looked at her watch. 'And in passing the car has a tankful of petrol.'

Lord George said respectfully: 'If you ever think of changing your profession—'

'Thank you.'

When they arrived there the pool was almost deserted, the attendants watching the clock for closing time, eager to reach their homes and a meal. Mario went straight downstairs to the changing rooms and the other three sat on a bench by the deep end. Opposite stood the guard and John Aldo, and Loretto was winding up for a flashy dive. Mario looked across at Charles Russell but gave no sign of recognition.

Mario de Var came up from the changing room and Aldo said something to the guard on his right. For a second he turned his head to answer and Mario slipped into the shallow end. He began to swim underwater towards the deep. Loretto ran the length of the board and dived.

Charles Russell raised a hand in command and Aldo mule-kicked sideways at the guard. Both knees went and he fell into the pool head first. He began to thrash furiously, sinking and coming up again, choking but still calling for help. An attendant saw him and went in after him. Aldo had walked round the head of the bath and joined the other three watching intently.

They weren't watching the attendant as he tried to drag the guard to the rail; they were watching a sort of shadow play, something they couldn't see in detail, two men below the surface struggling, moving in formal hieratic patterns.

De Var came up first and swam to the side. Molly gave him the overcoat but for a moment they lingered. The water had very slightly reddened, and presently Frank Loretto surfaced too. He floated belly-up, a dead fish, and in that belly, right of the navel and deadly, was the hilt of a knife but no sign of the steel.

In the car Molly Grant asked Russell: 'Where to?'

'Make for Maastricht and the Limburg border. I have very good friends in Holland.'

'We'll need them.'

17

The Prime Minister was telling Lord George, not smugly since he was never that, but with a permissable dash of satisfaction: 'You were right—they acted extremely fast.'

'The Brethren, you mean?'

'Who else? When the bath attendants had

pumped out that bodyguard the first thing he did was to ring to the States, and within hours our predicted power struggle was in gear. Two top Brethren have already died, a matter which the Americans are bearing with a notable fortitude. That was something which has happened before but there is also something else significant. We know that *Belinda* is loaded and ready to sail. Well, she hasn't; she's still in Vlamshaven.'

'Implying that the Brethren have put the whole plot aside till they find a new boss? Who conceivably may not like it and kill it dead?'

'That was how you foresaw it yourself.'

'Then happy ending,' Lord George said but added: 'Or is it? *Belinda* is loaded with high-grade nuclear waste. Which has been packed on the cheap in inadequate containers. A timebomb ticking away for half Europe. And *Belinda* is still in Vlamshaven.'

'But not for long. I've seen to that.'

'You've done it remarkably quietly.'

'I had the tools. Instead of having to board a Belgian ship, instead of having to call a Press conference and invoke what is foolishly called world opinion, I've simply blackmailed the Belgian government. And I did it through our man in Brussels.'

Lord George was astonished and openly showed it. 'But Sir Otto is hardly the man for tough talking.'

'In some ways you have Sir Otto wrong. Fortunately he's a dying type but it's one which has its own strange virtues. He's intensely patriotic in his very old-fashioned, unquestioning way... That a twopenny-ha'penny country like Belgium should have connived in such an outrage against his own! He went up in the air like a rocket and landed hard. And, of course, there was the personal factor too. Sir Otto was a deeply offended man. He was Her Majesty's ambassador, no less and if the coup had come off he'd have looked a great fool. He gave the Minister concerned a very rough ride indeed.'

'I wish I'd been there to hear it. What happened?'

'He started by saying that we know the whole story. We had only to slip it down to Vienna and Belgium would be in the dock with chains on. America would certainly back us and very probably Russia too. Not out of love but from something more powerful. Naked fear.'

'What happened then?'

'Sir Otto put the boot in with gusto.' This time the Prime Minister didn't mimic; he could do Sir Otto the caricature diplomat but not Sir

Otto the furious man. 'The Minister would no doubt remember that on a previous occasion he, Sir Otto, had made a suggestion. Belgium was known to have more nuclear waste than the capacity to deal with it safely. But Sir Otto's country was better than some at nuclear waste. Not outstandingly good but much better than Belgium. Moreover it had some spare capacity. So *Belinda's* load would be safely repacked and sent to England for proper treatment. That had been a suggestion once, now it was an instruction. Or else.'

...Or else what?

There was a body in Vienna called the International Atomic Energy Commission. And the Press of the world was by no means impotent.

...But this was blackmail.

Precisely that. And the services mentioned would come at a blackmailer's price.

Lord George laughed happily; he enjoyed a black joke. 'And what do you call a blackmailer's price?'

'How much do you think it was worth to Loretto?'

'Several millions at least to tempt him into it.'

'I thought the same and added some more. Moreover there'll be further consignments.'

Lord George said: 'Congratulations' and meant it. 'But at a less exalted level than yours, the sort of ground where I myself operate, I can see a snag. Or rather six snags.'

'Name them, please.'

'That bodyguard, Frank Loretto's body, stuck like a pig, Charles Russell, myself, de Var and Molly Grant. In short the whole affair at that swimming pool.'

The Prime Minister waved a dismissive hand. 'But all that was part of the little bargain. The easiest part as it happened in practice since the Belgian police were on the hook themselves. They could probably piece it together all right but if they did so they would expose their masters. So they haven't and won't.'

Lord George was looking doubtful still but the Prime Minister continued confidently. 'And apart from very strong hints from upstairs that no one is going to lose their stripes if this particular crime is left unsolved the Belgian police have a motive of their own to lay off. Frank Loretto had been dealing in drugs in Belgium; they had tried but they had failed to break him. Anybody who knocked him off would hardly be their Number One enemy. "Let justice be done though the heavens fall" isn't a maxim highly thought of in Belgium, or if it is it's a matter of theory.'

'You sound very sure.'

'Well, look what happened. The one man left in Belgium to help them was Frank Loretto's guard or hoodlum. They could have held him for ever as a material witness. Instead of which they rush him to Brussels and put him on the first flight to the States. Where, in passing, I wouldn't care to insure his life.'

'And Loretto himself?'

'Again they played ball. His wife slipped over and buried him quietly. She didn't want the body sent home where she might have had quite serious trouble in getting him buried with benefit of priest. He was a Catholic, of course—they all of them are—but he had got himself unpopular with his church. No, not because he dealt in heroin—there are worse sins than that and he'd committed both of them. He was a very rich man and he hadn't kicked in; he hadn't subscribed to, let's call them, the charities. Worse, he was an anti-clerical who'd made disparaging remarks in public. But his wife could find a priest in Belgium so he hasn't been interred with gangster pomp. He's buried in a public cemetery.'

'Which leaves Mario de Var, Charles Russell, myself and Molly Grant. We were all at the same hotel, the Royal George, and all of us at the pool that evening.'

'You're a stickler for tying the ends up, aren't you? So take Mario de Var first. The police will research him and discover his motive. Thereafter they'll privately drink his health. They don't like men like Frank Loretto, and as I told you they'll have been told not to break their backs.'

'And us three?'

'What of you? The only way to get you to Belgium would be to apply for warrants of extradition—the head of the Security Executive, its ex-head and the Prime Minister's personal adviser. You couldn't do that and keep it quiet. The Press on both sides of the Channel would jump at it and very soon you'd have the real story in headlines. Which is exactly what the Belgian government doesn't want.'

Lord George thought this over for some time; finally he asked: 'So you think we're in the clear?'

'I'm sure of it. We've had a bit of luck, I suppose, but as I see it this affair is closed.'

'So what do we do now?'

'Precisely nothing. You go back to your distinguished career as Russell will go back to retirement. As for John Aldo, at the lowest he has greatly obliged us. I like to pay my debts when I can so I've arranged that he may stay here permanently.'

'And Mario de Var?'

'There you go again! Unlike John Aldo he has no criminal record. I don't have to pull strings to let him stay here. If he wants to, that is, and I gather he does. He seems to be very thick with Molly Grant.'

'I'd very much like to buy you dinner.'

'A great pleasure but another time. I'm taking Sara out to celebrate.'

'I think I'll do the same with Laura.'

'An excellent idea. Good morning.'

Molly de Var rolled over and woke Mario. She knew he liked to rise early though she did not. 'I'll get the tea,' he said and went for it. They might have been married for years instead of days. When he came back she asked conversationally: 'So you'll never go back to Sicily?'

'Never. The de Vars are dinosaurs, dying because they can't adapt. I don't want any part of their decay.'

'Still, I'm sorry I shan't give you a son.'

'Why in God's name do I want a son?'

'The title,' she said.

'You know what you can do with the titles. The fancy Spanish ones will die with me. A good thing too—we never used them. But the old barony has female remainder and my eldest sister a healthy son. If anyone cares about that it will survive.'

They were living in her flat in Fulham and she knew that they wouldn't be begging their bread. She held a long lease on the comfortable flat; he had sent money to England before he'd left Sicily and what his English mother had left him had never left England. She herself would go on with her work but he must find it. He wasn't the type to take to well-heeled idleness. This subject she now brought up directly. She knew exactly what would offend him and what would not.

'Have you been putting out feelers about a job?'

'One or two. Unsuccessfully.'

'If you fancy it I've found you one. Lord George will very gladly take you on.'

'The Security Executive?' He sounded doubtful and she hid a wifely smile. She knew what he was thinking precisely. He would happily kill in a matter of honour but he wouldn't care to kill for money. Well, people had the oddest ideas, and on the subject of the Security Executive they were often more than odd: they were wholly wrong. She answered the question he hadn't needed to ask.

'They won't take you on because they know you've killed. In point of fact they hardly ever do that. It's regarded as inelegant, something to be invoked as a last resort. But you have virtues which will surely attract them.'

'Give me one, please.'

'You're not a liberal humanist, are you?'

'I'm not sure I'd care to define what that is.'

'Nor would I.' As a scientist she was wary of all definitions. By the time you had made the necessary exceptions the rule was in practice down to its underclothes. 'But I know one when I see one.'

'So do I.'

'And mistrust them?'

'Profoundly. I much prefer the honest realist, men like my godfather who deal in *realpolitik*. They haven't an illusion between them. And you'll remember I went to a Catholic school.'

'And subversion?' she asked softly. 'That's the Executive's daily meat and drink.'

'Define subversion.'

'Not bloody likely. You can't define an abstraction on principle.'

'*You* can't—you're too clever to try. But I can define a subversive and I will.' He poured the last of the tea and said reflectively: 'Society, unless it's based on blind caste, is held in one piece by the frailest of threads. Subversives come in all shapes and sizes from foolish rich

women with houses in Hampstead to the professionals who smear the police. Most are far
to the Left but a few are far Right.'

'You're going to do well in the Security
Executive.'

Charles Russell had returned from Soken-le-
Queen where he had arranged to meet Captain
Cole with a surprise. It had been a pair of
superlative London-made shotguns, for the
Prime Minister had thought it unseemly to let
Cole's services go wholly unrecognised. He had
once remarked in bitter jest that if Cole had
been a second-class actor or even a second-class
civil servant he could have arranged a CBE
very easily. But Cole was neither and would
be embarrassed by an unexplained and, in the
circumstances inexplicable, honour. So the
Prime Minister had consulted Russell.

A pair of really good guns, they had decided
—that was it. Captain Cole shot very little now
but the point of a pair of first-class guns was
that they were something you could hand down
as an heirloom. You might not use them much
yourself but a grandson would be proud to
show them off.

Russell had made the presentation gracefully
but had returned to Leastleigh-on-Sea a little
low. The change to retirement had not been

267

easy but he had made it with a conscious discipline. Now he had to do it again for an unexpected taste of action had rekindled a sharp appetite for a life which he had quietly relished. He was finding adjustment harder the second time. He never permitted the sin of *accidie*, knowing that if you did so you were lost. But this morning, for once, the time was dragging. It was two months after his visit to Belgium.

When the telephone rang he picked it up idly. It was probably some tradesman or other but instead it was a voice he had once known well.

'Colonel Charles Russell?'

'That must be John Aldo.'

'I'm established here in England for good. I wrote you a letter of thanks but that's not enough.'

'I started the machine, I suppose, but it was Lord George who drove it safely home. Where are you ringing from?'

'Soken-le-Queen.'

It was only a few miles away where what might have been a political crisis had started with illegal tipping. 'What on earth are you doing in Queens?'

'You don't mind?' The voice was close to apprehension.

'Of course I don't, but why pick on Queens? My money would have been on a flat in London.'

'I'm afraid you would have lost it, sir. Soken-le-Queen had exactly what I was looking for, a nice little Georgian house in the High Street.'

And probably not so little, Russell thought. 'You'll be bored to death in Queens.'

'I think not. I've bought a little business on the side.'

'Legitimate?'

'The local antique shop.'

'Then you'll lose a lot of money.'

'Maybe.' Russell knew Aldo could well afford to but the last thing he would do would be to mention it. 'Also I'm engaged to be married.'

'Sincerest congratulations.'

'Thank you. Also she's a local, which helps. Her family has been here for centuries and quite soon I'll be more than an eccentric American. Finally she wants children. So do I.'

'You must bring her over at once.'

'You mean it?'

'Of course I mean it. Will Sunday suit you?'

It didn't but Aldo said: 'You're too kind.'

'Come at noon for a couple of drinks before

luncheon. I'm very eager to meet you both.'

He hung up and poured a second sherry. 'Eager', he was thinking contentedly, was the biggest understatement of the year. Leastleigh wasn't a bad old dump: there were plenty of men he could chat to socially, even one who had served in his own battalion. But they hadn't led Charles Russell's later life and he missed its own peculiar friendships. It didn't much matter which side you were on, his own, the law's (or quite often outside it) or the other which had once been John Aldo's. His appearance at Queens was manna from heaven. Leastleigh held some pleasant people but so far not a defected Brother. Glory, glory, he'd have someone to talk to.

He called his housekeeper and made arrangements for lunch. *Boeuf stroganoff*, he rather thought. The local mushrooms were better than average and his housekeeper cooked rice superbly.